The Happy Hollisters and the Scarecrow Mystery

BY JERRY WEST

Illustrated by Helen S. Hamilton

GARDEN CITY, N.Y.

Doubleday & Company, Inc.

Contents

CHAPTER 1

MISSING!

BEEP! *Beep!*

Mr. Hollister blew the horn of his station wagon parked beside the rambling home on Pine Lake.

"Where are my helpers?" he cried. "*The Trading Post* opens at eight. Besides, I have a surprise!"

"Coming, Dad!" The screen door burst open and Pete Hollister raced out. Tall and well built for his twelve years, the blue-eyed boy leaped down the porch steps two at a time.

His sister Pam, ten, followed, her fluffy golden hair ruffled by the June breeze. She and Pete slid in beside their father, a handsome, athletic-looking man.

"What's the surprise?" Pam begged.

Mr. Hollister glanced at his lovely daughter, started the car, and grinned. "I finished the new invention at the store last night."

"The collapsible canoe?" Pete asked.

Mr. Hollister nodded. "It's just about ready to test," he said proudly.

"I can hardly wait to see it," Pam said as her

father neared *The Trading Post* in the center of Shoreham.

"Let us open the store for you, Dad!" Pete suggested.

Mr. Hollister smiled, stopped the car, and handed the boy his key case. The brother and sister hopped out while their father drove into an alley which led to the rear of the combined hardware, sports and toy shop.

The Trading Post was a one-story building with two large plate-glass windows and a door set between them. Pam glanced at the toys and sporting goods on display while Pete selected a large brass key and inserted it in the lock.

He grasped the handle. Then, even before he could turn the key, the door swung open under the pressure of his hand.

Pete gasped. "Pam! The door wasn't locked last night!"

Mr. Hollister had left the car and now approached the children. "What did you say, Pete?" he asked.

"Someone forgot to lock up," Pete said as he stepped inside, followed by Pam and his father.

"I used the key myself," Mr. Hollister said, puzzled. "I wonder if——"

Suddenly Pam cried out, "Dad! Pete! The store has been robbed!"

All three stood thunderstruck as they glanced down the long aisle which ran the length of the

6

store. Merchandise was strewn about, some of it knocked to the floor.

"Crickets!" Pete exclaimed. "The place was ransacked."

As the Hollisters hurried to the rear of the store, a sudden fear gripped Pam. "Dad!" she cried out. "Your new invention! The collapsible canoe. Do you suppose that's what the thieves were after?"

Mr. Hollister raced to a little room in the back of his shop. In it he kept tools for making minor repairs. It was here that he had worked the night before on his new invention.

As his children watched with pounding hearts, Mr. Hollister flung open the door. He sighed in relief. The canoe was there!

"Thank goodness!" he said.

"Then what *did* the thieves want?" Pete asked, glancing around the disordered counters.

At that moment two men walked in. "Indy! Tinker!" Pam called out. "We've been robbed!"

"What!" exclaimed the shorter of the two.

He was a stocky man of thirty-five and his jet-black hair, high cheekbones, and reddish-tan complexion marked him as an Indian. "Indy" Roades worked for Mr. Hollister as did Tinker, the man with him, who was tall, thin, and elderly. The two glanced about the shop in amazement.

"Quick!" Mr. Hollister said. "We must find out what was taken."

Everybody hurried from counter to counter, ex-

7

"Crickets! The place was ransacked!"

amining the misplaced goods as they searched to determine what had been stolen.

"Look here!" Tinker cried out, pointing to a rack containing picks and axes. Three of each were missing.

"They were all here when we closed up last night," Mr. Hollister said.

Indy, at the other end of the store, cried out, "Mr. Hollister!" The others raced to where Indy stood beside a table on which was a sign reading PROSPECTORS' MATERIAL. "Two of our best Geiger counters are missing!" the Indian said.

Mr. Hollister whistled softly. "Geiger counters, picks and axes," he said. "It looks as if some would-be uranium prospectors helped themselves."

"Shall I call the police, Dad?" Pete asked.

"Yes, son. Have Officer Cal come right away if he can."

Pete hurried to the office telephone and dialed the police department. He asked for Officer Cal, a young policeman who had helped the Hollisters solve other mysteries since they had moved to Shoreham. The lieutenant who answered informed Pete that Officer Cal was touring the town in a prowl car.

"Our *Trading Post* has been robbed!" Pete said.

"I'll send Cal over right away," was the answer.

The children waited anxiously. In a few moments a police car pulled up in front of the store and a good-looking officer stepped out. Hurrying into the store, he said, "The lieutenant contacted me by radio. You say you've been robbed. That's too bad."

"Some valuable articles were taken," Pete told him.

After hearing the story, Officer Cal said, "This looks like the job of two people." He began an examination of the premises. First he looked at the front door lock. "This is strange," he said. "It hasn't been forced."

"The thief used a key, you mean?" Pete asked.

"Apparently," came the reply. "But how they found one to fit is a mystery."

After learning what articles were missing, the policeman stepped inside his car and radioed headquarters. He reported the robbery, then added, "Send over our fingerprint expert."

"What can we do to help?" Pam asked, as Officer Cal returned to the store.

He suggested that they question local merchants who had opened their shops earlier that morning. "Ask them if they saw any suspicious-looking characters prowling around."

Pete and Pam eagerly took up the assignment. "Let's try the service station," Pete said. "It opens early."

Before they reached the gas pumps at the next corner they noticed two boys walking toward them. "Ugh, Joey Brill and Will Wilson," Pam remarked.

Joey, a frowning boy of Pete's age but larger, continually made trouble for the Hollisters. Will

Wilson, his friend, also played mean tricks whenever he saw the chance.

As the two boys approached, Joey cried out, "I just heard you reported a burglary at your place." He smirked. "What's the big idea of making up a story about a fake robbery?"

"It was no fake," Pam said indignantly, and Pete doubled up his fists. His sister nudged him and whispered, "Don't fight. Maybe Joey and Will can help us."

Pete got the hint. "Were you fellows around here early this morning?"

"We did go fishing about six," Joey remarked. "We passed your store on our bikes."

Pete asked the boys if they had seen anything unusual.

"Oh, sure," Joey continued. "A man standing at your store door."

"Are you certain?" Pam asked excitedly.

"Of course," Will added.

"We thought this fellow looked suspicious," Joey went on, "so we trailed him."

"Where did he go?"

"Into a house at 16 Walnut Street," Joey answered. "He went in and didn't come out."

"Thanks, Joey," Pete said. He and his sister hurried off. Walnut Street lay at the fringe of the business district and was not far away.

"Here's Walnut Street," Pete said as they turned a corner. "And there's number 16 across the road."

The children ran up the steps and rang the door-bell. A little old lady with gray hair and a sweet face, who held a cat under each arm, answered. After the children had introduced themselves, Pete said, "We're looking for a man who came in here about six o'clock this morning."

The old lady's eyes widened. "Came in here!" she exclaimed.

"That's what we were told," Pete said.

"Goodness, oh dear!" the woman said, wringing her hands. "It must have been a burglar. I'll go call the police."

"Wait, please!" Pam begged, trying to calm the agitated lady. "Doesn't a man live here?"

"Oh my no!" the woman replied. "I live here all alone with my cats."

"We're very sorry," Pete said, realizing that once again Joey and Will had played a trick on them.

As they were apologizing to the woman, some-body behind the Hollisters snickered. Whirling about, they saw Will and Joey standing across the street doubled over with laughter.

"You mean things!" Pam cried, and Pete went after them.

Joey and Will took to their heels and finally Pete gave up the chase. He and Pam asked for information about a suspicious-looking man from the gas station attendant and shopkeepers near *The Trading Post* but no one could help them.

When they returned to the store, the children

found a crowd gathered. "And there are Mother and the rest of the family," Pam said.

"Daddy phoned me the news," said Mrs. Hollister, who was slender and attractive-looking.

"Isn't it awful?" cried Holly. The six-year-old girl paused to retie the yellow bow on her left pigtail.

"Did you find any clues?" asked Ricky, who was seven. He had red hair, mussed as usual, and freckles on his nose.

When Pam shook her head sadly, her dark-haired four-year-old sister Sue tried to console her. "Don't worry. We'll catch the bad old robber," she said cheerfully.

"The police are working inside," Mrs. Hollister said, "and asked all of us to wait out here."

Just then Officer Cal and a plain-clothes man came out to report they had had no luck with the fingerprints.

"If we only had some kind of lead," Officer Cal said.

"Crickets!" Pete exclaimed and snapped his fingers. "I have an idea."

"What's that?" Officer Cal asked.

"Dad has the name of *The Trading Post* stamped on those ax handles."

Officer Cal jotted this information in a notebook.

"May we go back inside now?" Pam asked him.

Officer Cal nodded and went off in the police car. The children trooped into the store and looked about. Presently Sue ran up the center aisle, wearing a lightweight hunting cap. It was so large it nearly covered her eyes.

"Where did you get that?" Pete asked.

"I found it," Sue said, pirouetting.

"Where?"

"In the back of the store near the tents."

"Let me see it, please," the older boy asked.

Sue took off the hat and handed it to her brother. After examining it Pete excitedly called to his father.

"Dad, this isn't one of the hats we sell. The label states it's from a store in Montreal, Canada!"

CHAPTER 2

A CANOE RACE

"GOOD work, Sue." Pam smiled and bent down to kiss her little sister on the cheek. "You found a clue, honey."

As Sue beamed with delight, the hat was passed around for everyone to examine.

"I guess the name of the store in Montreal is the only clue," Mr. Hollister said.

"Maybe not, Dad," Pete said, looking closely at the inside of the hatband. "Something is written here in ink, but it's very faded."

"I'll get a magnifying glass," Mr. Hollister offered and hurried to his desk in the corner of the store. He returned with the glass and examined the faded writing.

"Can you make it out, John?" Mrs. Hollister asked her husband.

"Yes, I can, Elaine. The letters are F-r-e-n-c-h-y."

"Frenchy!" Pete exclaimed. "He must be the owner of the hat."

"Yikes!" Ricky exclaimed. "All we have to do is find Frenchy and we have the thief!"

15

"I suppose," said Mr. Hollister, "that this is a nickname for someone of French descent."

Indy spoke up. "The only 'Frenchy' I know is the fellow who runs Pierre's Bakery."

"But I hardly think he's the thief," Mrs. Hollister said quickly. "I often buy pastry at his store. He's a very nice man."

"Just the same we ought to investigate him," Ricky spoke up, trying to lower his voice so it would sound like a policeman's.

"All right," Mr. Hollister agreed. "Suppose you go to Pierre's while I send Indy to police headquarters with this cap."

Pam took Sue by the hand and the five children hurried from *The Trading Post* and down the street.

"I can smell the bakery," Holly said a few minutes later.

The enticing aroma of pies and cakes grew stronger as the children turned into the small shop. Pierre, wearing a white baker's hat, came from a back room carrying a tray of sugar buns. He was a short man with a round face and a small waxed mustache.

"Yes?" he said, lifting his eyebrows.

"Do you have a Geiger counter?" Ricky blurted out.

Pierre looked puzzled. He slid the tray of buns into the showcase and waved his hands expressively. "I have lemon meringue pie and éclairs and special strawberry tarts, but none of these what-you-call-it."

"Do you have a Geiger counter?"

"Please excuse my brother," Pam spoke up. "He shouldn't have said Geiger counter."

"Oh," Pierre said, and looked relieved. "Geiger is down the street. He has a shoe store. No, I didn't buy my counter from him." He took a cloth and wiped the marble counter before him with a flourish.

Pete grinned. "I'm afraid you don't understand. What we want to know, is your name Frenchy?"

The baker beamed. "They call me that," he said.

"And you come from Montreal?" Ricky went on.

"No, no, no, from Lyon, many years ago. *Oui*, a fine city," he said, blowing a kiss in the direction of France.

This made all the Hollisters smile. "Pierre," asked Pete, "are there many fellows in Shoreham with the nickname Frenchy?"

"*Oui*," the baker replied, rolling his eyes. "Nearly everybody here from France or French Canada is called Frenchy."

Ricky continued his impatient quest for clues. "Where were you last night, Pierre?"

The baker pointed to the back room. "In there," he said, "mixing crumb cakes and apple pies and butter rings. Now," he said, wiping his hands on his apron, "what would you like?"

Pam felt embarrassed and her hand reached into her skirt pocket. There was a fifty-cent piece tied securely in her handkerchief. She had saved it to go to the movies that afternoon.

"We'd like seven sugar buns," she said.

18

Pierre reached into the tray and separated a section of the warm buns. "I'll give you eight for the price of seven," he said, beaming. He slid the buns into a white bag and handed them to Pam.

She paid him, then the children returned to *The Trading Post* and told their parents that Pierre was not the Frenchy for whom they were looking.

At this moment a tall, fine-looking man walked into *The Trading Post*. He was well built, middle-aged, and had neatly combed gray hair.

"Is Mr. Hollister in?" he asked.

"I'm Mr. Hollister," the children's father said as he stepped forward.

The man offered his hand. "I'm Mr. Tucker. Damon Tucker. Your brother told me about a new collapsible canoe you've invented. Mr. Hollister, may I see it? If I like the canoe, I may purchase several."

Mr. Hollister introduced his family, then said that the canoes were not yet for sale. The model had to be given severe tests.

"It will be ready to try on Pine Lake here tomorrow," he said. "Then it will need a final test in rapids."

Mr. Tucker looked surprised. "You have rapids in Shoreham?" he asked.

"Oh no," Mr. Hollister replied.

The caller went on. "I know just the place for you to test the canoe—at my forest hunting preserve. It has a lake and a river with rapids." He turned to the children. "You'll be interested in this. The

19

lake is called Fox Lake because it's shaped like a fox."

"Oh, how 'citing!" cried Sue. "Does the fox have legs?"

Mr. Tucker laughed. "Yes, it does. And out of one of its front legs runs the river. There are rapids in it, so we called it Whirlpool River."

"It sounds lovely!" Pam exclaimed.

"The preserve is called Spruce Forest," Mr. Tucker went on. Then his eyes twinkled. "I have an idea, Mr. Hollister. Why don't you take your family on a camping trip when you test the canoe? There's an excellent camp site on the back of the fox!"

"Oh let's go!" Holly begged.

"Yikes!" said Ricky. "Is it wild in Spruce Forest, Mr. Tucker?"

"As uninhabited as the moon," the man replied, chuckling, "except for the forest animals."

Mr. Hollister thanked the man for his kind offer, but said he doubted that they could make the trip at this time.

"Well," Mr. Tucker went on, "if you change your mind, let me know. I'll be at the Shoreham Hotel. Please keep me advised about your canoe. I'm interested in knowing how the tests come out. Good-by."

After Mr. Tucker had left, the Hollister children looked pleadingly at their parents.

"It would be wonderful to go camping," Pete

20

said. "And we could try out some of the new equipment you're selling in the store, Dad."

"And I want to see the little forest animals, Daddy," Sue spoke up.

"Me, too," Holly chimed in, twirling a pigtail.

Mr. Hollister said he did not like to disappoint them. "Perhaps we can make the camping trip later in the summer," he added. "But first we must test the canoe on the lake. We'll do it tomorrow."

For the rest of the afternoon the Hollisters played along the shore front of Pine Lake, rowing their boat and throwing sticks into the lake for their collie dog Zip to retrieve. For a while Sue busied herself dressing up White Nose the cat and her five kittens, Midnight, Snowball, Tutti-Frutti, Smoky and Cuddly. But the chief topics of conversation among the children were the possible camping trip to Spruce Forest and the burglary at *The Trading Post*.

That evening the telephone rang and Pam ran to answer it. Officer Cal was calling.

"I have some news for you," he said. "An ax with *The Trading Post* stamp on it was found near a gas station in the town of Glendale. The proprietor said it must have dropped out of a car which had stopped there for fuel."

"Oh thank you," said Pam. "I'll tell Dad."

After she relayed this information to her family, the girl took an atlas from the living-room bookcase. Opening it, she located the town of Glendale.

"Crickets!" Pete shouted. "It's near Spruce Forest!"

Pam showed the map to her parents.

"So it is," Mrs. Hollister said. "And look! It's only fifty miles from that newly discovered uranium field we were reading about."

"Jumping catfish!" Mr. Hollister cried. "The thieves who stole the Geiger counter probably are heading for that place."

Ricky looked triumphant. "Now we *have* to accept Mr. Tucker's offer," he cried.

"Yes," Pete agreed. "We could test the canoe in the rapids and look for the thieves at the same time."

Mrs. Hollister smiled at her husband. "The children have a point," she said. "I think I'd like to make the trip too."

"Oh Mommy, I love you!" Holly cried, throwing her arms about her mother.

"We'll do it!" Mr. Hollister said. "I'll call Mr. Tucker now."

That night the happy Hollister children dreamed of rapids and woods and campfires. Pete found himself chasing Joey who had taken Pierre's hat and was selling buns to Mr. Tucker! He awoke with a grin.

After breakfast next morning Mr. Hollister and Pete drove to *The Trading Post* and returned with the collapsible canoe. They carried it to the dock. The canoe had ribbed aluminum sections which

22

folded up like an accordion, and it could be carried in a small space. After pulling the release levers on the ends, they watched the canoe elongate section by section. Next Pete and his father tightened the little screws under the gunwales, so the canoe would not collapse while in water.

By this time the other children had arrived and Pete said, "Dad, please let Pam and me test it."

"All right. Step in."

Pete took the stern position and his sister the bow. Mr. Hollister handed them paddles and they started off. The canoe, being of aluminum, was extremely light and glided along swiftly.

"This is keen!" Pete shouted.

Suddenly he spied Joey and Will coming toward them in Joey's wooden canoe. It pulled alongside the Hollisters.

"What a funny-looking tub," Joey scoffed.

"It's faster than yours," Pete retorted.

"Oh yes?" said Will. "We'll challenge you to a race!"

Pam called, "Whoever reaches our dock first wins. One, two, three, go!"

Paddles flashed as the four contestants raced their canoes across the lake. Inch by inch Pete and Pam pulled ahead of their opponents. Joey and Will were hopelessly beaten as Mr. Hollister's new canoe sped toward the dock.

"We win!" Pam, turning to her brother, who was

still paddling hard. "Stop!" she warned. "We'll hit the dock!"

Pete tried to swerve the canoe as the rest of the family watched breathlessly from the wharf. But the metal craft was so speedy that the boy could not act in time. He tried to backwater, but it was too late.

Thump! The canoe smashed into the dock!

CHAPTER 3

A BULLY IS DUNKED

THE force of the impact pitched Pam out of the canoe and onto the dock. She skidded along on her knees until her father caught her and lifted his daughter up.

At the same time the lever in the canoe broke in two and the front section of the aluminum craft telescoped. Pete, who had lurched forward, hung onto the gunwales. The water rushed in through the open seams and the canoe sank to the bottom in four feet of water.

Adding to the consternation of the Hollisters was the derisive laughter of Joey and Will. Instead of lending a hand to Pete, who ducked beneath the surface to retrieve the canoe, Joey shouted, "Ha, ha, what a phony invention!"

"Yeah!" Will added. "We win the race because you sank." Smirking, the bullies paddled off.

Pam, meanwhile, was looking down ruefully at two skinned knees.

25

"Are you all right except for your knees?" her mother asked anxiously. When her daughter nodded, the two hurried into the house to bathe Pam's bruises and apply bandages.

Mr. Hollister and Ricky helped the dripping Pete pull the canoe onto the dock. There was a dent in the bow, but aside from that and the broken lever the canoe had withstood the crash very well.

"I'm terribly sorry, Dad," said Pete. "Can you repair it?"

His father said yes. "And I'd better make a stronger lever."

"Let me help you," Pete volunteered.

Together they carried the canoe to the station wagon and drove off to Mr. Hollister's repair shop at *The Trading Post*.

While they were gone Ricky said to Holly and Sue, "If we're going to Spruce Forest, we ought to practice camping."

"Where?" Holly asked.

"Right here in our own yard. We can make a tent."

Ricky ran to the garage and came back with a piece of rope. Quickly he tied each end to the branches of two small apple trees which stood about ten feet apart near the lake front.

"I know what we can use for a tent," Holly said eagerly. "Sue, let's get that old blanket from the attic." They hurried off.

26

When the girls returned with the blanket, Ricky flung it over the taut rope and tied each of the four corners to sticks which he pounded into the ground.

"Hurray! We have a tent!" Sue cried out as she ducked beneath it.

Her brother and sister crawled in after her and Zip poked his head inside too. Holly suddenly gasped, for held tightly in the dog's jaws was a squirming frog.

"Zip, you're naughty," she said. "Here, give it to me!"

She took the frog from the dog's mouth. The cool green creature was unhurt and Holly carried him back to the lake front. He jumped into the water with a splash and disappeared among the reeds.

"Oh Zip, I don't know what to do with you," Holly said, as she crawled back into the tent with the others. "I know you like to catch frogs, but you might hurt them."

The collie dog whined softly, putting his long nose between his damp forepaws.

"All right, if you're sorry," Sue said. Then she wagged a finger at their pet. "But don't do it again."

Ricky laughed. "Wait until Zip gets on the trail of real wild animals in Spruce Forest! Say, let's pretend we're in Spruce Forest right now. Zip and I will go out scouting for the burglars while you girls mind the tent."

When Holly and Sue agreed, the boy scrambled

"Help."

outside and disappeared into some bushes with Zip at his heels.

"What'll we do now?" Sue asked Holly.

Holly's eyes brightened as her eyes fell on the tent rope. "Let's play we're on a train. I'll pull the cord for an emergency stop."

"Oh good!" Sue remarked. "You'll save us from a train wreck."

Holly nodded and, reaching up, pulled the old rope. *Snap!* The rope broke and the blanket fell on top of the two girls.

"Ugh! Ow! Help!" they called as they thrashed around.

On the other side of the bushes Ricky heard the commotion. "Come on, Zip! Someone's calling for help," he cried, dashing back toward the tent.

When the dog saw the wriggling mass on the ground, he broke into furious barking. Ricky pulled the blanket off Holly and Sue. Now that their surprise was over, they burst into giggles.

"Oh Holly!" Sue said. "You tried to save us from a train wreck, but you wrecked us instead!"

By this time Zip had trotted back to the cattails along the shore, evidently to look for more frogs.

As Ricky finished putting up the tent again, he glanced across the water and made a wry face. "Look, girls, they're back."

Holly and Sue turned. Joey and Will were paddling toward the Hollister dock. Nearing it, both

29

boys put down their paddles and picked up bows and arrows from the bottom of the canoe.

Sue clutched Ricky's arm and whispered fearfully, "Do you suppose they're going to shoot at us?"

"I'll ask them," Ricky said and shouted, "Say, fellows, what're you going to do with those bows and arrows?"

"Shoot frogs," Joey replied, and Will added, "There're lots of them around your dock. See, Zip's barking at one now."

"You shouldn't shoot frogs!" Holly cried out.

"We'll shoot them if we want to," Joey declared. "Now all of you stand back from the shore so you won't get hit."

"I think you're mean, Joey Brill!" Sue called out. "Frogs are nice and you shouldn't hurt them."

"Stand back, I said," Joey commanded as he fitted an arrow to his bow string.

"Look! I see one over there," Will said, pointing among the reeds.

On a rock sat a large frog, sunning himself. Joey stood up cautiously, planting one foot on either gunwale of the canoe.

"I'll get a better shot at him this way," he said, pulling on the bow string.

Holly clapped her hands over her eyes. She could not bear to see what was going to happen.

Suddenly Ricky looked up into the air and cried, "Oh, see that funny airplane!"

Joey instantly glanced up too, but in doing so he lost his balance.

"Hey! Help!" he cried as the canoe teetered first one way, then the other.

The bow and arrow flew from his hands and Joey tumbled into the water! Will clutched at the sides of the canoe but could not hold the craft steady. It tilted and filled with water, dumping Will into the lake beside his friend.

Holly giggled at the sight and Sue said, "That's good. And now the frog's gone."

When Joey and Will stood up and grabbed the canoe, they spluttered and shook their fists at the children on the dock.

"I'll get you for this, Ricky Hollister!" Joey cried out. "There wasn't any airplane at all!"

Ricky looked meek. "It must have been a bird I saw," he said.

Joey glared at him. "Now I *will* shoot all the frogs I want to," he threatened, as the two boys climbed back into their canoe.

As both paddles and the bows and arrows were floating some distance from the canoe, Joey and Will started paddling with their hands to reach the spot.

"We can get Mother and make them stop," Holly said nervously.

"I have a quicker plan," Ricky said. "Here, Zip!"

The dog trotted over and Ricky whispered "Fetch" into his ear, and pointed out on the water.

Immediately the collie jumped into the lake and swam swiftly toward the floating arrows. As he came to each one he snapped it up in his jaws, then raced for shore as Joey and Will howled in dismay.

"Hey! Give us back our arrows!" Joey demanded as he and Will retrieved their bows and paddles.

"Only if you promise to go away from here and not bother the frogs," Ricky said as Zip dropped the two arrows at his feet.

"Okay, we'll promise," Joey said, paddling toward the dock.

When they came alongside, Ricky dropped the arrows into the wet canoe. Zip looked on, growling quietly.

"Let's get away from here quick," Will urged. "I don't like that dog."

"He won't bother you as long as you don't invade his frog hunting ground," Holly told him.

Glowering in defeat, the bullies paddled swiftly out of sight. The Hollisters, grinning, turned back to the tent. "I hope they don't bother us any more," said Sue.

"Let's have some more camping-out practice," Ricky said, then added hopefully, "Maybe we can sleep in our tent overnight."

"Oh, that would be fun!" Sue squealed.

A short time later Pete and his father returned from *The Trading Post.* "We fixed the canoe," Pete said. "It's stronger than ever. We can still take it on our trip to Spruce Forest."

At this moment Pam came from the house. She had entirely recovered from her accident, although her knees were covered with bandages. She and Pete and their father laughed when they heard what had happened to Joey and Will.

Mr. Hollister told the children that he had stopped at police headquarters and learned that the captain had sent out a seven-state alarm for the men who had stolen the Geiger counters.

"There's no sign of them so far," he added.

"I'd sure like to get on the trail of those burglars," Ricky said. "Maybe we can find a clue at Spruce Forest."

After supper the children asked permission to sleep out in their homemade tent, as practice for their camping trip. Mr. and Mrs. Hollister exchanged glances. Then the children's mother said, "All right. You can see how you like being outdoors all night."

As it grew dark the children put on their pajamas, unrolled their sleeping bags, and lay down side by side in the tent. Sue was the first to fall asleep.

Finally Pete saw the lights in their home go out. Zip, he knew, was in his favorite spot alongside the kitchen range. Now it was completely black and the only sounds were from the chirping crickets and the grandfather bullfrogs' "ka-zooming."

In the middle of the night Pam stirred. She had heard a noise. What was it? Propping herself on her elbows, the girl listened. There, it came again. A thud on the side of the tent.

Pam's heart raced. What was happening? Suddenly another thud and something rolled down the side of the tent!

CHAPTER 4

THE PANCAKE GIRL

THIS time Pete awakened. "What's going on?" he asked, reaching for the flashlight beside his head.

"Somebody's throwing something at our tent," Pam whispered. Now all the other children had awakened. An owl hooted in the distance.

"Oh!" Holly gasped. "Can't you find out who's out there, Pete?"

Her brother wriggled from his sleeping bag and poked his head out of the tent. *Thud!* Something hit him on the head!

"Crickets!" Pete yelled. "It's an apple!"

"They're falling off the trees!" Pam laughed in relief.

"Who's afraid of an apple?" Ricky shrugged. "Let's go back to sleep!"

Awakening again at daylight, the children rolled up their sleeping bags and slipped quietly into the house to dress. When they came downstairs again, Pam noticed a note on the kitchen table.

"Dear children:" it read, "You'll probably be up ahead of Daddy and me and very hungry. Here are directions for making pancakes. Let us know when they are ready."

"Yikes! Mother sure is smart!" Ricky said admiringly. "How did she know we'd be hungry?"

Pete suggested that they cook the pancakes on a grill they had built on the water front.

"Come on, Ricky," Pete urged, "we'll build a fire."

While Ricky made a bed of paper and twigs, Pete gathered up larger pieces of wood. Soon a good fire was crackling under the grill.

In the kitchen, meanwhile, Pam had assembled a box of pancake mix and other ingredients. Consulting the directions, she said, "First I add milk to the flour, then an egg and some melted butter."

While Pam mixed the flour and milk, Holly measured out the butter and melted it. Sue beat the egg. Then the girls took turns stirring the mixture.

"We're nearly ready," Pam announced. "Holly, you take the griddle and paper plates out to the grill."

"I'll carry the batter," Sue proposed, reaching high for the bowl on the kitchen counter.

Crash! The container slipped from the little girl's fingers and fell to the floor. Batter flew in all directions, covering Sue from head to toes!

"Oh!" she exclaimed. "I want to cry but I can't 'cause my eyes are full of pancakes!"

Pam's heart sank as she gazed at the ruined batter, but she said kindly to her little sister, "Stand still,

Zip licked the batter off Sue's face.

honey, and I'll wipe you off." She reached for a towel.

Hearing the noise, Zip nudged the screen door open and came inside. He immediately began to lick the batter off Sue's face!

At this moment the children heard footsteps coming down the back stairs and Mrs. Hollister appeared. "My goodness!" she said.

"I'm terribly sorry," said Sue, as her mother took her upstairs for a shampoo and bath.

Meanwhile Pam and Holly mixed another bowl of batter. The boys came into the kitchen.

"Our fire is just about ready for the flapjacks," Pete announced.

"And we're ready," said Pam.

Soon the family was gathered at the shore front, and crisp, golden pancakes were giving out a tempting aroma from the griddle. Ricky was especially generous with the powdered sugar and maple syrup. "Yum!" he said. "These are wonderful."

Oranges and hot cocoa, which Mrs. Hollister had provided, added to the delicious breakfast, during which conversation turned to the trip to Spruce Forest.

"Dad," Pete asked, "is there uranium in Mr. Tucker's game preserve?"

"I never heard of any," Mr. Hollister replied, "but perhaps we should take a Geiger counter along and do some prospecting of our own. Suppose I take you all to *The Trading Post* this morning to pick out our camping equipment."

This suggestion was greeted by cheers. When the paper plates had been burned in the fire and the utensils taken back to the house, it was time for Mr. Hollister to set off for *The Trading Post*. When he and the children arrived at the store, Tinker and Indy were already there.

The Indian said good morning, then added, "Officer Cal was here a few minutes ago. He thinks the Geiger counter thieves are hunting for uranium near Glendale."

Ricky was joyful. "We'll find them!"

Mr. Hollister smiled and said, "Then the sooner we set off the better. Indy, help us select our camping equipment. First on the list will be tents."

"We just got the new shipment yesterday," Indy said. "They're called the explorer type."

Indy showed them the tents, which were held up by poles front and back, the one in front being higher and having a crossbar. He explained that the tents were lightweight, easy to put up, and provided maximum room. He suggested that the campers take three of them: a large one for Mr. and Mrs. Hollister, the next smaller size for the three girls, and a still smaller one for Pete and Ricky.

"Yikes!" Ricky exclaimed. "We'll have a village of tents."

The Hollisters now selected the rest of their camping equipment. This included hatchets, cooking utensils, a special bottled gas for the stove, and air-filled mattresses. Pete picked out an especially sensitive Geiger counter.

Rickey asked if he might have a new radium-dial wristwatch. "So I can tell time in the dark."

Mr. Hollister agreed and Ricky chose a sturdy one.

All the gear was stowed in the back of the station wagon and taken to the house. "I guess we can start tomorrow, Elaine," Mr. Hollister told his wife.

"What about our pets?" Pam asked.

"I think we should take Zip along," her father suggested. "He may be of assistance to us in the woods."

"He can scent the thieves' trail!" Ricky cried excitedly.

It was agreed that the Hollisters' cats would be placed in charge of Jeff and Ann Hunter, playmates of the Hollisters who lived nearby. Holly ran over to make the arrangements.

The rest of the day was taken up with packing for the trip. Mrs. Hollister took care of the food supply while Pam supervised the selection of suitable clothes for the children: shorts, shirts, slacks, and rugged hiking shoes.

Next morning Holly took the kittens to the Hunters' home. When she returned the car was packed. The tents had been stowed in a special rack on top of the station wagon and the car seemed to bulge with baggage. Sue decided to carry her doll but set

40

her tiny suitcase alongside the others. Zip was the last passenger to bound in and jumped to the back seat. Then the door was slammed shut.

"We're off to Spruce Forest!" Holly cried.

Mr. Hollister announced that they would spend the first night at a motel en route. At five o'clock they reached it. They found that the place had a restaurant where they enjoyed a delicious roast beef supper topped off with apple pie and ice cream. The travelers went to bed early and were up at six o'clock.

As they drove out of the motel grounds after breakfast, the proprietor came up to the car. "Did you sleep well and enjoy your stay?" he asked.

"Very much," Mr. Hollister replied.

"Where are you folks heading?" the man inquired.

"Spruce Forest."

"I wish you luck!"

The proprietor's tone of voice aroused Pam's curiosity. "Why will we need luck?" she asked.

"Well," the man replied, "there are mighty, mighty strange doings around that area."

Mrs. Hollister tried to question him further, but he seemed reluctant to say any more. Waving, he walked off.

"Crickets!" Pete exclaimed. "We may be in for some real excitement!"

Most of the morning was taken up in speculation about what lay ahead of the Hollisters in Spruce

Forest. They stopped for an early lunch and about two hours later came to the outskirts of a small town.

Ricky was first to spot a sign. "Dad! This is Glendale!"

Mr. Hollister drove along the main street, bordered by stone and frame houses, to the business center. This comprised a cluster of stores around a small square, with one house at a corner. On it was a sign reading: E. D. RICE, M.D.

"He's probably the town doctor," Pam guessed.

"And there's a filling station!" Peter cried. "Maybe it's the one where the thieves dropped our ax!"

Mr. Hollister pulled up beside a gasoline pump and blew his horn. "Fill the tank," he said when the attendant, a smiling young man, came out of the garage.

As the gasoline gurgled through the hose, Mr. Hollister identified himself as the owner of *The Trading Post* and asked, "Is this the place where our stolen ax was found?"

"Yes, it is, sir."

Pete spoke up. "What did the thieves look like?"

"They appeared to be hunters," the young man replied. "I thought this was odd because it's off season."

"Did they have guns with them?" Ricky asked.

"I saw two in the back seat."

"How did the ax fall out of the car?" Pam queried.

The attendant explained that the fellow sitting

42

in the right front seat got out to pay for the gasoline. "I saw several axes and a couple of queer-looking gadgets on the floor of the car," he said.

"Geiger counters!" Ricky declared.

"Come to think of it, I guess they were," the young man went on. "When the man got back into the car, one of the axes must have slid to the pavement. I didn't notice it until after they'd left."

The full nozzle clicked off and the attendant screwed the gas cap back on. As he pulled a cloth from his back pocket and started to wipe the windshield, Mrs. Hollister said, "Was there anything unusual about these men to help us identify them?"

The young fellow paused thoughtfully for a moment. "The man who paid the bill," he said, "had very bushy black eyebrows. They made him look sort of—fierce." Sue shuddered.

"What direction did they take?" her father asked as he pulled out his billfold.

"That way," the man pointed. "Toward Spruce Forest. But I don't suppose they stopped there. Mr. Tucker never lets anybody on his game preserve except by special permission."

"We're going there!" Sue piped up with a pleased look.

"Have a good time," the young man said, smiling.

As Mr. Hollister pulled out onto the road again, Holly leaned out of the window. "Let us know if you ever see those bad men again," she called.

"I sure will," the attendant replied.

Fifteen miles farther along the travelers saw a rustic sign reading: SPRUCE FOREST. An arrow pointed down a narrow rutted road. Trees grew so close to the road on both sides that leaves brushed against the car as Mr. Hollister drove along it.

Holly, reaching out to snatch a few leaves from the branches, said, "It's getting spookier all the time."

Her mother was glancing at a map unfolded on her lap. "I think this road leads to the shore of Fox Lake," she said. "In fact, it ends right on the fox's back."

They had gone only half a mile when suddenly the ragged-looking figure of a man with arms outstretched appeared some distance ahead. He stood in the middle of the road.

The children gasped and their father quickly applied the brakes. As he did, two words echoed ominously through the forest:

"Go back! Go back!"

CHAPTER 5

A STRANGE NICKNAME

THE Hollisters were startled by the strange warning. Everything was quiet for a moment until the voice repeated, "Go back! There's danger in Spruce Forest."

"Maybe we'd better go back," Holly said nervously.

Pete looked defiantly at the odd figure far down the road. "Nobody's going to scare us away," he said. "Come on, Dad, let's find out who this fellow is."

The children's parents agreed that they should not leave until they learned what authority the ragged man had to chase them away.

"We do have Mr. Tucker's permission to camp here," Mr. Hollister said. "Pete, get the binoculars from my suitcase."

The boy reached over the back seat of the station wagon and unzipped his father's blue traveling bag. The binoculars lay on the top. Pete handed them forward.

Immediately Mr. Hollister trained them on the

45

"Let's try to find out where the voice came from."

figure in the road. The children watched him intently and were amazed to see a grin come over their father's face. He put the binoculars down and chuckled.

"That's not a man at all. It's a scarecrow!"

The others laughed, then Holly asked, "But how can a scarecrow talk?"

"Someone's playing a trick on us, I guess," Pete surmised.

"But why should he?" Pam asked. No one could answer this.

Mr. Hollister proceeded slowly toward the scarecrow. Approaching it, he saw that the road was wide enough for him to skirt around the figure. As he did, Pete said:

"Dad, let's stop and try to find out where that voice came from."

Mr. Hollister stopped the car and they all got out. Zip bounded into the undergrowth, barking happily. Pete and Pam examined the tattered scarecrow which was stuffed with straw. There was no recording device on it.

"Maybe a loudspeaker was hidden in the bushes," Ricky said as he explored the roadside.

When nothing could be found, Mrs. Hollister called the children and Zip back to the car. Sue was the last to get in. As she shut the door, Pam noticed that the little girl held a piece of wire in her hand.

"Where did you find that?" Pam asked.

"By the side of the road," replied Sue, who already was shaping the wire in circles to make a bracelet for herself.

"Sue's found another clue," Pete said. "Let's look around some more."

The family made a thorough search of the area but could find no other evidence of a recording machine. Mrs. Hollister thought that perhaps someone had broadcast the warning, then picked up his equipment and disappeared into the woods.

"But Mr. Tucker said nobody lived here," Ricky reminded his family as the car started off again.

"I guess," said his father, "we've run into a real mystery."

"I hope we can solve it before we leave Spruce Forest," Pete remarked hopefully.

As Mrs. Hollister studied the map in her hands, her husband drove carefully along the trail. It became even more overgrown with trees and vines. Finally they came to a rise of ground covered with pine trees. Here the road ended. Beyond lay a sparkling lake.

"Here's a wonderful place for a camp," Pete said.

His father agreed that the site was cool and beautifully located and looked as if it had good drainage.

"How about it, Elaine?" he said.

"A perfect spot," Mrs. Hollister answered.

As the children stepped out onto the ground, they found it covered with pine needles. Ricky and Holly slid down the slope to the lake front, Zip at their heels.

"There's been a camp here before," Holly cried out. Nearby were the remains of a campfire.

The children raced back to the others and told them. Mr. Hollister frowned. "There's no question but that others use this forest."

Mrs. Hollister nodded, but said calmly, "It was probably Mr. Tucker himself, so there's nothing to worry about."

In the excitement of setting up camp the children temporarily put any mysterious stranger out of their minds. The air was fragrant with the scent of pine. Though the sun was hot, the tall trees provided cool shade.

The tents and bedding were quickly removed from the top of the car. Mr. Hollister and Pete selected an open place under the trees to pitch the tents. Meanwhile Mrs. Hollister and the three girls busied themselves unloading the clothing and food supplies while Ricky set up the portable gas stove in front of his parents' tent.

"Yikes!" Ricky cried out when he finished his job. He ran back to the station wagon, pulled out the collapsible canoe, and leaned it against a clump of bushes near the water. Then he got his fishing tackle.

"Who'd like fish for supper?" he called out as he threw his line into the water.

"Catch us a muskie," Mr. Hollister replied. "I hear the lake is full of muskellunge."

After Sue had helped her mother as much as she could, the little girl wandered off among the pine trees. Two minutes later she screamed, then hurried back to the others, crying: "A scarecrow! A live scarecrow!"

"What!" Mrs. Hollister exclaimed as the frightened child threw herself against her mother.

"I saw a scarecrow and it was walking!" she exclaimed.

The others glanced in the direction where Sue was pointing. A gasp went up from the family as a man emerged from among the trees.

He looked very much like the scarecrow they had seen on the old road. The fellow had a full, white beard, a thin nose, and small, beady eyes. A tattered shirt and jeans and a battered straw hat on his head gave the stranger a ludicrous appearance.

"See, I told you, he's a scarecrow!" Sue whispered.

The man said nothing but continued to approach them slowly.

"Who are you?" Mr. Hollister called out.

The man removed his straw hat and held it in his hands. "Scarecrow is my name," he answered. "At least that's what people call me."

Mrs. Hollister spoke to the old man kindly. "But what is your real name, Mr. Scarecrow?" she asked.

"That's nobody's business," the old fellow replied tartly, gazing from one to the other.

"Can we help you?" Mrs. Hollister asked kindly. "We have food if you would like some."

50

Without replying to her question, Scarecrow looked directly at Mr. Hollister and said, "If you stay here, you'll be in real danger. I advise you to go back."

"That's what you told us before, didn't you?" Mr. Hollister asked him.

At this the old man appeared startled. "I've never seen you before."

Pete spoke up. "Didn't you throw your voice back on the road near the real scarecrow?"

"What scarecrow?" the old fellow said, perplexed.

Pete told the man what had happened on their way in from the highway.

"I don't know anything about it," the old fellow grumbled.

"If you're in trouble, we'd like to help you," Mrs. Hollister repeated. Her kind words seemed to penetrate Scarecrow's rough exterior.

"Thank you," he said. "I don't need any help, but I'm warning you. Go back where you came from before you get into trouble." With that he turned on his heel and strolled off into the woods.

"He's a strange one," Pete said as the elderly man disappeared.

Mrs. Hollister seemed more concerned than her husband. "John," she said, "we may really be in danger. Perhaps it would be advisable to return home."

Her husband shook his head. "I don't think the old fellow will harm us," he said. "He's probably only an eccentric hermit."

"Still, we'd better be on the lookout," Mrs. Hollister advised. "He may be warning us about some other kind of danger."

Pam hunched her shoulders. "It's going to be spooky with Scarecrow prowling around."

Ricky snapped his fingers. "What say we follow him and find out where he lives?"

But the boy's parents did not think this was a wise move. "If Scarecrow is a hermit," Mrs. Hollister said, "he probably wants to be left alone. If he doesn't bother us, we shouldn't follow him."

As the other children discussed the strange man, Holly wandered down to the lake front where Ricky had left his fishing line. She picked up the pole and jerked the lure which lay on the surface far out in the water. Instantly there was a tremendous splash. The pole was nearly pulled from Holly's hands.

"I've caught a fish!" she screamed and tried to reel in the big catch which now thrashed furiously in the water.

But the fish was so strong that it pulled out more line, making the reel hum as the handle spun about.

"Hang on, Holly! You've got a whopper!" Pete cried, dashing to her assistance.

"It's a muskie!" Mr. Hollister called out. "Hang on tight!"

Holly was so excited that she grabbed the fishing line with both hands and started to pull in the leaping fish. Before Pete could reach her, the line became tangled around her wrist. The muskellunge gave a terrific jerk.

"Help!" Holly cried as she was pulled into the lake.

CHAPTER 6

TRAIL BLAZERS

"HELP! Help!" Holly continued to cry as the big fish pulled her through the water.

Pete ran to the lake edge and plunged in. Fifteen feet from shore he reached his sister, unloosed the line from her hands, and wrapped it around his own wrist. Then with Holly helping him, he yanked the muskie along. When they reached the dock, Mr. Hollister also grabbed the line and together the three pulled in the big fish hand over hand.

"That's a funny way to catch a fish," Pam said, giggling, as Ricky helped wrestle the large brown and green muskie from the water. It had a long snout and large, sharp teeth.

"Careful!" Mr. Hollister warned. "Don't let it bite you."

"No wonder that fish pulled Holly in," Ricky said. "It's nearly as long as she is."

Their father said this muskie was the largest he had ever seen caught. "It's a prize, Holly. What a meal it'll make!"

The girl laughed, then she and Pete changed to

54

dry clothes. Meanwhile Mrs. Hollister heated the skillet and Ricky and his father cleaned the fish. Then it was cut into pieces and dropped into the frying pan.

"Mum! It smells 'licious," Sue remarked as the aroma of frying fish drifted through the camp.

Later, as the family ate supper, Mrs. Hollister said, "The best I've ever tasted."

That evening the boys built a campfire near the lake and the family sat around it, talking of the strange events of the past few days. Then, as Zip dozed, Mr. Hollister told the children stories about the woods.

"If you hear strange noises in the night, don't be alarmed," he said. "The woods animals will probably come to investigate us."

Sue's eyes widened as she said, "I hope a bear doesn't snoop around here, Daddy."

He told her not to worry, saying that sometimes people camp out for years without ever seeing a bear. "Once in a while a man will notice claw marks on a tree," Mr. Hollister said, "but Bruin doesn't venture near people if he can help it."

"What does a bear track look like?" Holly asked.

Her father picked up a stick and made an outline of a bear's paw on the ground. The toe marks were separated from the rest of the footprint. "I doubt that a bear will visit us," Mr. Hollister said. "And now to bed, everyone."

"How about Scarecrow?" Ricky asked as the children inflated their mattresses. "Maybe he'll come prowling around tonight."

"If he should," Mrs. Hollister answered, smiling, "he'll have Zip to reckon with. We'll tie the dog to a tree near the tents."

In a short time everyone retired. The last flashlight was switched off and all was quiet except the low whispers of the children. Soon the Hollisters were asleep, and Zip had flattened out on the pine needles and was drowsing in the moonlight.

Holly did not know how long she had been sleeping when she was awakened by the low whine of their pet. She quickly roused Pam, and Sue awoke too. The older girl peered out of the tent opening.

Seeing nothing, Pam flashed her light about. "There it is," she whispered, as the beam fell on a fast-moving animal. It disappeared in the direction of the shore.

"Let's follow it," Holly suggested eagerly.

She unzipped the netting at the front of the tent and the three girls crept out.

"Quiet, Zip," Holly said in a low voice.

Sue grabbed Pam's hand. "It—it's not a bear, do you think?" she asked.

"The animal wasn't large enough to be a bear," Pam replied.

When they reached the lake front Holly said, "Look! There are his tracks in the soft ground."

Bending low, the children examined the marks.

"Is it a bear?" Sue asked, trying to recall the design her father had made earlier in the evening.

Pam looked more carefully and saw that the toe marks were not separated from the rest of the footprints like a bear's. Besides, the marks were small.

They led along the edge of the water. The girls followed them. Suddenly Pam said, "How cute!"

Seated on a log was a raccoon. The light shone directly in his eyes which glowed like tiny lamps.

"So you were our prowler!" The girl laughed.

"I'll bet he was trying to get some of our food," Holly remarked.

"Sure he was," Sue added. Then she called, "Take off that mask, Mr. Raccoon. We know you."

The little animal stared at them for a few minutes, then ran into a small cave among some rocks. The girls waited for a few minutes, but the reccoon did not reappear.

"We'd better get back to bed," Pam suggested.

At breakfast next morning the girls told their story to the others. Ricky said instantly, "I would have gone right into the cave to get that raccoon!"

"You couldn't. It's too small," Holly told her brother.

Mr. Hollister explained that raccoons' dens are usually in hollow trees, but sometimes they live in small caves. In either case, he said, the den would not be far from the water. "That's because most of a raccoon's food consists of frogs, turtles, mussels, or fish."

"And doesn't a raccoon wash all his food before he eats it?" Mrs. Hollister asked.

"That's the common belief," her husband replied, "but some woodsmen say the raccoon's food is wet because he gets it from the water, not because he's especially dainty."

"Let's look for more animal tracks," Pete proposed when they finished eating.

Mr. Hollister told him they would probably find some near the shore and they all walked to the edge of the lake. The raccoon's tracks which led directly to the animal's den were very plain.

"Here are some others," Pete called out. "What are they?"

After examining them closely, Pam said, "They look like a cat's tracks."

Mr. Hollister chuckled. "That's the kind of cat you want to stay away from," he said. "These marks were made by a skunk."

He pointed out that the skunk had five toes instead of four like a cat. "And besides, a skunk is quite pigeon-toed."

"I'm glad Mr. Skunk didn't visit our tent," Ricky said, holding his nose and giggling.

"If he ever does, don't disturb him," Mr. Hollister warned. "Well, what would you all like to do this morning?"

"Shoot the rapids," said Ricky.

"I'm not ready yet to do that," his father said. "I want to test the canoe in calm water first."

"So you were our prowler!"

"Then let's go animal hunting," Pete suggested.

"You children might do that. Don't go far, of course."

"Suppose we get lost in the woods," Holly remarked cautiously.

Mr. Hollister said they could easily overcome that problem. He directed Ricky to go for a bag in the compartment of the station wagon. When the boy returned with the package, his father opened it and reached inside. He pulled out a handful of yellow disks, a box of tacks, and a small hammer.

"I get it!" Pete cried. "These are for blazing a trail, aren't they?"

"Right," his father replied. "Using these disks is the modern way to blaze a trail."

He explained that tacking colored markers on trees was easier than cutting off pieces of the bark. "Besides," Mr. Hollister added, "each trail blazer uses a different-colored disk in case one trail should cross another. This avoids confusion and keeps the traveler on the right path."

The children listened eagerly as he went on to tell them something of the old type of trail blazing.

"Old-time woodsmen cut a slash on either side of a tree as they went along. This acted as a guide on their return or directed anyone else who wished to follow the trail. A blaze made on the side of the tree, but closer to the ground than usual, meant the person was to turn there. Three short blazes down

60

the center of a trunk was a warning. This mark was commonly used by trappers."

Ricky grinned. "Just like markers on the highway, eh, Dad?" he asked.

"Exactly. A long blaze cut vertically in the center of a tree trunk and another long mark made horizontally alongside it indicates the direction of a camp or cabin."

"I feel like an old woodsman already." Pete grinned as he took the yellow markers and put them in his pocket.

"Dad, may I carry the Geiger counter?" Holly requested before they started out. "Maybe we can find uranium." When he nodded, she hurried to the station wagon to get it.

"If you hear it click," Mr. Hollister said, smiling, "you'll know you've discovered a treasure!"

It was decided that Sue would stay with her parents. Eagerly the other four children set off into the woods close to the lake shore. Zip frisked along at their side. Reaching a marshy spot, the little group turned directly into a denser section of the woods. At intervals Pete would hand Ricky one of the yellow disks which he tacked onto a tree.

After they had gone a quarter of a mile, looking right and left for animal tracks, Holly said, "Please, may I tack up some of the yellow circles, Ricky?"

"Sure," the boy answered. "I'll carry the Geiger counter."

He handed the hammer and tacks to his sister and

took the box in his right hand. After carrying it for a while this way, he shifted it to his left. Suddenly as he crossed a pile of rocks, the Geiger counter began to click furiously.

Ricky stood stock still. "Listen!" he cried.

The others crowded around. *Click! Click!*

"Yikes!" the boy shouted. "We've discovered uranium!"

CHAPTER 7

A LOBSTICK MESSAGE

"URANIUM for the government!" Pete said. "What a discovery!"

Holly jumped up and down excitedly. "Hurry! Let's tell Mother and Dad," she cried.

She tacked three of the yellow disks onto a tree beside the pile of rocks. Then Pete took the Geiger counter from his brother, whistled for Zip, and the children raced back toward camp. The blaze marks clearly showed the way, so it was not long before the brothers and sisters arrived at the pine tree clearing.

Mr. and Mrs. Hollister were extending the collapsible canoe on the lake shore. They looked up, startled, as the breathless group burst upon them.

"We found some!" Ricky shouted.

"Come quick and see," Holly urged them.

"Please, children, one at a time!" Mrs. Hollister said. "What did you find?"

"Uranium!" Pete exclaimed and told about the clicking of the Geiger counter.

"I had a hunch there might be uranium around here," his father said, grinning.

Taking Sue with them, Mr. and Mrs. Hollister

tramped through the woods after the other children. Zip barked happily as he raced along, flushing a rabbit here and there in the bushes.

When they reached the pile of rocks," Pete held the Geiger counter and said, "Sh! Listen!"

There was not a sound.

"Maybe if you shake it, the counter will start clicking," Holly suggested.

Pete did this, but still there was no response.

Mr. Hollister grimaced and said, "Are you children teasing Mother and me?"

"Honest, Dad. It clicked before when I held it," Ricky said.

"Then suppose you show us exactly what you did," his father said.

Ricky took the Geiger counter from his brother and held it in both hands over the rock.

Click! Click! Click!

"See, I told you!" the boy said, his eyes dancing with excitement.

"Let me try it," Mrs. Hollister spoke up.

But when she held the Geiger counter, it was silent again.

Suddenly Pam giggled. "Oh, I know what happened! Ricky's wristwatch has a radium dial. That's what made the counter click!"

They all looked amazed for a moment, then started laughing.

"I guess the joke is on all of us," Pete said. "Oh well, we may find uranium yet."

Mr. and Mrs. Hollister and Sue returned to camp. The others continued their hike for a while, seeing many tracks of deer but none of any other animals. The children turned back. Upon reaching their tent site, they saw their parents and Sue bringing the canoe to shore. When the family was together, Ricky said:

"What's that funny thing in front of your tent, Dad?"

A split stick had been driven into the ground. Mr. Hollister said he knew nothing about it and all hurried over to examine the stick. In the crotch was a piece of bark on which was scratched a message.

"Leave Spruce Forest!" It was signed J.B.

"Joey Brill!" Ricky shouted. "How did he get up here?"

"Maybe he's trying to get even with us," Pete said, "for making him fall out of his canoe."

Mr. and Mrs. Hollister and Pam did not agree that the initials were Joey's.

"Well, somebody sure is trying to get us to leave Spruce Forest!" Pete said indignantly. "Do you suppose it's that Scarecrow man?"

"It might be," Mrs. Hollister answered thoughtfully. "He wouldn't tell us his real name, so these might be his initials." Turning to her husband, she said, "I'm becoming a bit worried, John. Do you think we should stay here?"

Mr. Hollister said that as long as Mr. Tucker had invited them to come to the preserve there could be no real danger. "Maybe it's someone's idea of a joke," he suggested.

"Well, it's a funny way to leave a message," Sue spoke up.

"This is an old forester's trick," her father explained. "The split stick is known as a wilderness post office. Sometimes it's called a lobstick."

"But the message doesn't have a stamp on it," Holly declared.

Mr. Hollister smiled and said that letters left in the wilderness post office need no stamps and are not sealed in an envelope either.

"Whoever finds a message on a lobstick," he said, "reads it, then passes the information along to the person for whom it's intended."

"Maybe this one's not meant for us," Pam suggested.

"I'm afraid it is, since there's no other name on it," her father said. "But we're not going to pay any attention to the note."

Holly, who never remained too serious for long, suddenly said, "Let's play wilderness post office!"

"Okay!" Ricky agreed. He took out his knife, cut a small branch from a nearby sapling, and put a neat slice in the top of it.

While he pounded the stick into the ground, Holly found a piece of bark and worked to scratch the word "Sue" on the back of it.

Meanwhile Pete and Pam walked to the lake front

where the canoe rested on the shore. "May we take a ride?" Pete called to his father.

"All right, but be careful."

"We will."

The two children shoved the craft into the water. Pam took the forward paddle while her brother seated himself in the stern. With graceful strokes they sent the canoe gliding over the mirrorlike lake. Neither Pete nor Pam had ever seen such clear water before. They could look straight down to the pebbly bottom across which a fish occasionally wriggled.

"Let's paddle to the other side of the lake and back again," Pete suggested.

At this point Fox Lake was about two miles wide. When the children reached the opposite shore, they noticed many coves with sandy beaches. As Pete guided the canoe around a little point of land, a large crane splashed out of the water directly ahead.

"Oh!" Pam said startled, as the lovely bird rose high over head.

"Look!" Pete said in a hushed voice.

Near the end of the cove a mother deer and two fawn walked gingerly to the edge of the water and lowered their heads for a drink. The two children rested their paddles on the gunwales and watched silently. When the deer turned and walked back into the woods, Pam said:

"Isn't it wonderful to be in a real wilderness, Pete? This is just like it was when the Indians lived here."

Pete guided the canoe under the branches of a tree which overhung the shore. "Let's cool off a moment in the shade," he said.

Suddenly Pam whispered excitedly, "Look Pete!" She pointed along the shore.

Another canoe came gliding toward them. Two strange men were in it, their bodies bent forward as they paddled strongly.

"Who do you suppose they are?" Pam whispered.

Pete replied that they looked like woodsmen.

"Do you think they saw us?" the girl asked.

"No. We're too well hidden," Pete said. "Don't move," he cautioned.

The men reached the shore two hundred feet from where the children watched. Without a word they stepped from the canoe. The taller of the two men picked it up and swung the craft over his head. In a moment they disappeared into the woods.

"Say Pam, maybe they are part of the mysterious goings-on in Spruce Forest," Pete said as they waited for a moment.

"Or maybe they had something to do with the burglary at Dad's store," Pam suggested.

"Let's follow them and find out who they are," said Pete impulsively.

"Perhaps we ought to tell Mother and Dad first," Pam replied.

But Pete thought that immediate action would be better. "We may lose the men's trail completely if we don't follow them now," he said.

"Do you think they saw us?"

Pete touched the water lightly with his paddle, sending the canoe out of its hiding place.

"We must be very careful," Pam warned as they neared the spot where the two men had landed.

She stepped out first and pulled the bow of the canoe up on the sandy shore. Then Pete leaped to her side.

"I think we'd better hide our canoe in the bushes over there," he said, "just in case the men are thieves."

The two children picked up the light craft and concealed it in a wild blackberry thicket. They tip-toed into the dense pine woods, with Pete leading the way cautiously.

"Do you see any blaze marks?" Pam asked her brother.

The boy looked at each tree as he came to it but saw no sign of marks cut into the bark.

As the children walked deep into Spruce Forest, Pam said, "I think we'd better blaze our own trail, Pete. Otherwise we may not be able to find our way back to the canoe."

"Good idea," he agreed and pulled a penknife from his pocket.

Pete flipped open a shiny blade. As the two children went on, he cut a small nick on both sides of various trees. A hundred yards farther on, the trail of the two men became fainter, and presently disappeared in a deep woodland stream.

"Now what'll we do?" Pam asked as she gazed among the dense trees.

"We ought to go a little farther," Pete said. "Perhaps those fellows have a camp near here."

They decided to follow the brook northward. Pete continued to cut more blaze marks as they walked deeper into the woods. The trees became taller and sunlight penetrated only here and there in slanting rays.

"It sure is spooky," Pete said as he stopped to listen.

"And I have a strange feeling that someone is looking at us," Pam said, glancing about fearfully.

"I guess we've come far enough now," her brother decided. "Maybe we can bring Dad back with us later and search farther."

The two children started to retrace their steps, being careful to follow the blaze marks. They had not gone far when suddenly a voice commanded:

"Stop!"

Pete and Pam froze in their tracks. Then they whirled around to face a boy of about fourteen. He was a handsome lad, dressed in buckskin trousers and a blue shirt. He had a square chin, a short, straight nose, gray eyes, and thick, black curly hair. His expression was serious as he gazed straight at the Hollisters.

As Pete got over his surprise, he said, "Hi! Are you camping here?"

When the boy seemed reluctant to answer, Pete asked, "What's your name?"

The lad shook his head. "I can't tell you."

"I'm Pete and this is my sister Pam."

"I know," the stranger answered, a tiny smile coming to his lips. "You're camping on the other side of the lake. Did you get my message?"

Pam looked startled. "The warning in the lobstick?"

"Yes, and I hope you take my advice."

"Why should we leave the woods?" Pete asked. "What's the danger?"

"I wish I could tell you but I can't," the boy replied, opening and closing his fists nervously.

"Is Scarecrow causing all the trouble around here?" Pete prodded.

The boy shook his head. "I can't say. Please don't ask me any more questions."

"If you're in trouble, perhaps we can help you," Pam said, feeling sorry for the stranger.

The lad stepped forward with a beseeching look in his eyes. "Please go away before they hurt you. If you don't——"

Just then a gunshot reverberated through the forest. Without another word the boy turned and fled into the woods.

CHAPTER 8

A FOREST BABY

PETE and Pam looked at each other astounded, as the echo of the gunshot died away and the strange boy disappeared from sight.

"What do you make of it, Sis?" Pete asked.

"I think the boy wanted to tell us something but didn't dare."

"It's certainly a mystery," her brother agreed.

The children returned to the spot where their canoe was hidden, all the while discussing the strange gunshot. Was it a signal for the boy to return? Or, if one of the strange men had fired, what was he shooting at?

As Pete and Pam quietly launched the craft into the water, Pete said, "I wonder what the boy's name really is?"

"We'll just have to call him J. B. until we find out," his sister replied as she dipped her paddle into the water.

When she and her brother reached camp, they

quickly pulled the canoe onto the shore, then ran to tell their family what had happened.

"Well, this is an unexpected turn of events," their father commented. "I don't like it."

Mrs. Hollister said she felt sorry for the boy. It was possible he needed protection. "Did you notice anything particular about J. B. which might give a clue to his identity?"

"His hair was very long," Pam observed. "It looked as if he'd been in the woods for so long he hadn't had a chance to get a haircut."

"You may come across him again," Mr. Hollister spoke up. "In any case I'm glad we're across the lake from the people who are using rifles."

Pete and Pam suddenly noticed that the younger children were not around. Their mother said Ricky and the girls had taken a fresh supply of yellow blaze marks and set out along the trail they had made earlier.

"They should be back any minute," Mrs. Hollister went on. "They weren't going far. Come and have some lunch. The rest of us have eaten."

The two children finished their meal. When fifteen more minutes had gone by and Ricky and his sisters had not returned, the Hollisters became worried. Pete and Pam offered to follow the well-marked trail to look for them.

"I'll go along," Mrs. Hollister said. "John, suppose you guard the camp. And anyway, the children may return by another route."

74

He agreed and the others hiked off. After going a quarter of a mile, glancing left and right, they failed to find Ricky, Holly, and Sue.

"I wonder how far they went?" said Pete.

Suddenly Pam noticed three yellow blaze marks tacked to a tall pine tree. Beneath them was a little mark pointing to the right. "Look!" she cried. "Ricky and the girls set off on another trail!"

The yellow disks clearly marked the new direction. It led up a slope, over the brow of a small hill, then down the other side. Soon the searchers came to the top of a steep, stony cliff with only a few scrubby bushes and trees growing on the upper section. Then the precipice became a solid wall of stone.

Cupping his hands to his mouth, Pete called out. His shouts were answered by a bark from Zip somewhere in the woods at the foot of the cliff.

"Holly! Ricky! Sue!" Pam shouted. "Where are you?"

"Down here," came Ricky's voice from deep in the thicket below.

"Are you all right?" his mother asked anxiously.

"Yes."

"Where are you?" Pete yelled. "We can't see you."

At the same moment Pam leaned as far over the cliff as she dared. About thirty feet below she saw some bushes moving. "There they are," she said. "I wonder——"

Suddenly the girl's feet slipped on a mossy stone. She plunged forward, rolling down the side of the cliff. Frantic, Pam grabbed at the scrubby growth. But it was not until she was about halfway down that she was able to grasp a sapling. It bent almost double under her weight.

"Hold on!" Pete cried, as he and his mother cautiously edged down the steep slope.

Bushes which they held onto uprooted easily and they slid dangerously. The two soon realized they could not safely reach Pam.

"Oh dear, this is dreadful," Mrs. Hollister murmured.

Pam, meanwhile, hung on desperately to the sapling. Her feet thrashed about, as she tried to get a foothold on the side of the precipice.

"I—can't—hold—on—much—longer!" she gasped breathlessly.

Just as the situation seemed hopeless, the faces of Ricky, Holly, and Sue peered up from the foliage below. Seeing their sister dangling from the sapling, they cried out in alarm.

Then Ricky had an idea. "Drop straight down, Pam," he suggested. "We'll catch you!"

The three children and Zip gathered in a tight knot directly beneath Pam and stretched up their arms.

"All right. Here I come!" she called, realizing that the roots of the sapling were about to pull out.

Pam let go and dropped to the bottom of the cliff. She landed squarely on the others. The force knocked the three children to the ground and her head bumped against Zip's back.

"Are you all right down there?" Mrs. Hollister cried out.

"Yes."

"Stay there until Pete and I can reach you."

Mrs. Hollister and Pete inched their way down a section of the cliff which was not so steep and finally reached the others. Outside of a few scratches and a red welt under Ricky's right eye, the children were all right. Even Zip showed no ill effects of the bump from Pam's head.

"Whew! That was a close one!" Pete said. "Tell me, how did you three get down here?"

Holly said they had walked along the marked trail and suddenly Ricky had noticed an old blaze mark which led to the right of their path. They followed it, looking carefully for more blazes. Since the marks were nearly gone, the children had posted their own disks on top of the original cuts.

"We thought it might lead somewhere important," Sue spoke up.

"But your trail ends on the top of the cliff," Pete said, pointing up.

Holly declared that they had become so excited at this point that they had forgotten to tack up their own blaze marks. Ricky and his two sisters had

77

"It's losted."

worked their way down the far slope to the bottom of the precipice.

"And that's when we discovered it!" said Sue proudly.

"Discovered what?" Pam asked.

"It's a secret, but we'll show you," the little girl answered.

With Zip dashing on ahead Ricky led his family to a secluded spot. It was surrounded by a ring of rhododendron bushes. In the center lay a tiny fawn.

"Oh, it's adorable!" Pam said, bending down to pet the little animal.

"It's losted," remarked Sue, "so we're going to take it home with us."

Mrs. Hollister wondered if this would be wise. "Maybe we'd better leave the fawn here until its mother comes," she suggested.

"Oh, but we can't," Holly said. "One of its legs is hurt."

Pete examined the little animal and discovered that its left hind leg was cut. "Maybe we should take the fawn to camp," he said, "because some wild animals might attack it."

"All right," his mother agreed.

Pete picked up the fawn and held it close to his chest. "Won't Dad be surprised when we return with this?" he said, chuckling.

Holly pointed out the old blaze mark on a nearby tree and the Hollisters had no difficulty following others like it. They scrambled up the slope until they came to their own yellow-disked trail.

Pete and Pam took turns carrying the fawn. By the time they reached their camp site, Pam was at the rear.

"Hello there!" Mr. Hollister said. "I thought all of you got lost!"

"Oh no!" Sue replied. "We found a s'prise. He's losted from his mother."

Pam hurried forward, the fawn in her arms. "Isn't he cute?" she said.

"A fine little animal," her father said.

Mrs. Hollister had already gone into her tent to get the first-aid kit. She quickly treated the fawn's leg.

"Now both of us have bandaged legs," Pam told the unfortunate animal.

Holly carried the baby deer into her tent and laid it on her sleeping bag. Soon the little creature fell asleep.

The children peeked in at their new pet many times during the afternoon between dips in the lake.

When the deer awakened just before supper, Sue ran for her doll's nursing bottle. "Our new baby needs to be fed!" she told the others. "Let's give him some milk, Holly."

A cupful of powdered milk was prepared and the small bottle filled. Then Holly, holding the fawn in her arms, inserted the nipple in the animal's mouth.

80

"Look! He's drinking it!" Sue exclaimed happily as the others looked on.

After the fawn had drunk, the Hollisters let it wander about the camp, hobbling on its bandaged leg.

"Look, Mother! He's not running away," Holly said. "Wouldn't it be fun to take him back to Shoreham?"

Sue, who sat cross-legged on the pine needle ground, did not think they should. Cupping her chin in her hands, she said worriedly, "But the poor mother deer, I know she'll miss her baby."

The discussion about whether or not to take the little animal to Shoreham went on well into the supper hour. But no decision was reached.

Later, when they were seated around the camp-fire with Zip and the fawn inside the circle, Mr. Hollister said, "Those old trail marks you children found when you discovered the fawn interest me."

"We thought maybe they would lead to something important," Ricky said. "That's why we followed them."

Mr. Hollister glanced at his wife. "Elaine," he said, "perhaps we can pick up that trail in the morning. It will be a good hike."

"Oh goody, Daddy, may we go, please?" Holly asked excitedly.

In the flicker of the firelight Ricky suddenly stared off into the darkness. "L-look at that!"

From out of the velvety blackness two eyes glowed luminously at them!

Holly shivered a little. "A wildcat!" she exclaimed.

Zip growled and was about to spring forward when Pam grabbed his collar. At the same time Mr. Hollister pulled a flashlight from his pocket and aimed it toward the woods. The beam revealed a lovely doe standing quietly and looking at them. She did not move.

"Can she be the little fawn's mother?" Pam asked excitedly.

"It's possible," said Mrs. Hollister. "If she has come for her baby, she should have it."

Zip growled again. Instantly the deer turned about and leaped into the blackness of the woods.

"She's gone," Pam said, disappointed, "and may never return."

Mrs. Hollister, however, thought that the doe would come back. "We'll put her baby near the spot where she stood and then pay no attention."

Pete picked up the tiny animal, walked toward the woods, and set it on the spot where the doe had vanished. Then they all returned to the campfire, Pam still holding Zip firmly.

The Hollisters sat gazing at the fire and listened. Presently they heard a rustle.

"Don't look now," Mrs. Hollister whispered. "We may frighten the doe away again."

The expectancy sent little chills of excitement through the children. When they had waited for five minutes, Mr. Hollister said, "Now let's see what happened."

CHAPTER 9

SCARECROW'S HIDEOUT

As HIS family waited tensely, Mr. Hollister beamed the flashlight toward the wood.

The tiny fawn had vanished!

"The doe really was its mother," Sue cried, clapping. "Now we can be the Happy Hollisters again!"

Even Zip held up his head and panted softly as if he were smiling over the reunion. Before the girls fell asleep in their tent they said a little prayer for the fawn and its mother, asking that the pair should reach their forest home in safety.

When the children arose next morning, Mr. and Mrs. Hollister already had bacon sizzling in the frying pan.

"All set for the big adventure?" Mr. Hollister asked after the children had taken a dip in the lake and eaten their breakfast.

"Yes," they chorused and Pete remarked, "Dad, maybe the old trail will lead us to those mysterious men Pam and I saw."

"And J. B. too," Pam said.

They had donned slacks and high walking boots

to protect themselves from the underbrush along the trail. Their knapsacks were packed with food and first-aid supplies.

"Let's go!" Mr. Hollister said. He and Zip led the way.

When they reached the cliff over which Pam had fallen the day before, Mr. Hollister turned left, then descended the hill and picked up the old blaze marks again.

"We seem to be heading in the direction of the lake," he observed as they trudged through the shady pine woods.

The trail turned left again and paralleled the lake front about a hundred yards from shore. In a little while they came to a clearing and Sue said, "Somebody made a lot of stumps!"

"I'll say he did," Mr. Hollister replied, smiling. "And he must have had several helpers."

At the far end of the clearing stood the ramshackle remains of an old sawmill and its broken-down bunkhouse. Next to the mill was a huge pile of sawdust.

"We've discovered an old logging camp," Pete declared, rushing forward.

Weeds and grass had grown as high as the weathered stumps.

Pete started to step over a fallen log which was covered with fungus. As he did, Holly, directly behind him, cried, "Pete, look out!"

On the log lay a snake, sunning itself. His multicolored skin blended with the bark and fungus, so that he was well protected.

The snake struck but missed the boy by inches. Then it slid off the log and disappeared among the weeds.

"Crickets! This place is dangerous!" Pete said as he thanked Holly for warning him.

Mrs. Hollister advised the children to proceed more cautiously every step of the way.

"Let's explore the old sawmill," Ricky proposed.

They approached the ancient circular saw which lay on its side, rusted and bent. The roof of the shed had caved in and the supporting timbers stuck out grotesquely.

"This place has been abandoned a long time," Mr. Hollister said.

"Judging by that pile of sawdust," said Pete, "they must have cut up a lot of timber."

He skirted the edge of the huge pile, his shoes sinking into the soft material. When he reached the far side of the mound, Pete stopped suddenly and glanced down.

"Footprints!" he shouted. "And they're not ours."

His father hurried to the spot, the others following him. "Somebody has been here recently," he declared.

"Then we'd better be careful," Mrs. Hollister remarked. "Those men Pete and Pam saw might be hiding in the old shack."

The children began to talk excitedly, but Mr.

Hollister raised his hand for silence. Everyone listened intently. Even Zip stood still, his ears pricked up.

A low moan came from inside the shack.

"Somebody's in there," Pam whispered. "Let's help him."

"Careful!" her mother warned. "This might be a trap."

Pete grabbed Zip's collar and approached the doorway cautiously. The front of the shack had sagged and the door stood ajar, hanging by one hinge.

"Hello inside!" Pete cried. There was no reply. Then the low moan was repeated.

Ricky stood manfully erect and called, "Come out of there! We have you surrounded!"

"Perhaps the person can't move," Pam said. "He may be injured."

"I'll go in first," Mr. Hollister said and slipped through the doorway.

The children and their mother pressed closely behind him. Inside it was gloomy and musty-smelling. A rickety table stood in the middle of the room. On the far side were four bunks.

"There's a man," said Pam in awe.

In the lower bunk on the left side lay a figure partly covered with a blanket.

"It's Scarecrow!" Pam cried unbelievingly.

The old man looked up at them with a dazed expression.

"What's the matter?" Mrs. Hollister asked. "Are you ill?"

"My leg," Scarecrow said. "It hurts!"

A small window in one wall let enough light into the shack for Mr. Hollister to examine Scarecrow's leg. It was swollen from his ankle to his knee.

"The leg looks as if it might be broken," the children's father said, then added, "Scarecrow, what happened to you?"

Mrs. Hollister interrupted. "Let's give him a cup of hot coffee first," she said. "The poor man is probably hungry too. He'll feel more like talking after he eats."

She opened her knapsack, pulled out a thermos bottle, and poured a cup of hot coffee. Scarecrow pushed himself up on one elbow and drank it. Then he nibbled on a ham sandwich which Mrs. Hollister offered him.

"Thank you," he said. "I was hungry and thirsty too, but I couldn't move to get a drink."

After he had revived somewhat, Scarecrow told them what had happened to him. He had gone for a log from a pile of wood behind the shack. But as he lifted it, one of the big logs had rolled down and hit his leg.

"I couldn't walk on it and barely managed to drag myself back here and get in the bunk," Scarecrow said. "Then the leg started to swell."

"Do you live here?" Pam asked, and Scarecrow nodded.

88

Sue took hold of his hand and said, "We'll help you, won't we, Mother?"

"We certainly will," Mrs. Hollister replied. "Pam, did you bring our first-aid kit?"

"Right here, Mother." The girl pulled it out of her knapsack.

Mrs. Hollister applied antiseptic lotion to a gash in Scarecrow's leg. Then she made a salty wet dressing and skillfully bandaged the leg.

"We'll have to get you to a doctor immediately," she said.

"You mean you'll carry me out?" the old fellow asked, his small eyes widening.

"Of course," Mr. Hollister answered with a grin. Glancing about the cabin, he spied an overcoat hanging from a peg on the wall. "We can use that, Pete. Bring it over here, please."

Mr. Hollister ripped a loose board from one of the other bunks. Then, taking Pete's belt hatchet, he split the wood down the center. As the children watched their father in admiration, he slipped the poles through the armholes of the coat. Then he tied the ends of the garment to the poles with a piece of rope he found on the floor.

"Crickets! That's a keen stretcher!" Pete said.

Scarecrow smiled. "Good thing I'm not heavy."

Pete and Pam laid the stretcher on the floor, then assisted their parents in moving Scarecrow from his bunk to the overcoat.

"All set!" Mr. Hollister said.

He carried the end of the stretcher nearest Scarecrow's head. His wife and Pete each took hold of one of the poles at the rear.

"I want to help too," Ricky complained as they moved through the front door.

"You'll have a chance," Mr. Hollister said.

After they had walked several hundred yards, Mr. Hollister called a halt. When they had rested several minutes, he took up his position again while Pam spelled her mother and Ricky relieved Pete.

During one of these pauses they ate the picnic lunch. It was late afternoon when they arrived at camp.

Scarecrow said that he felt much better and would wait until morning to see a doctor. "You're very kind to do this for me after the gruff way I spoke to you."

Pam smiled down at him. "We're always glad to help other people," she said.

Ricky ran for his air mattress and laid it on the ground outside his tent. Scarecrow was transferred to it and declared the mattress was much more comfortable than his bunk in the shack.

He watched the children have a swim, then joined the Hollisters in an early supper of grilled ham, potatoes, and peas. As dusk dropped down over the lake and forest, Pete bathed Scarecrow's leg and applied a new dressing, while Ricky and Holly built a roaring campfire.

They took turns carrying the stretcher.

"Do you feel well enough, Mr. Scarecrow," Sue asked, "to tell us some woods stories?"

"I'd be glad to."

Pete and his father carried the old man near the fire and propped him up against a stump. The glow of the fire made Scarecrow's beard look pink and white.

Sue walked up to him and looked straight into his eyes. "Are you Santa Claus's brother?" she asked.

For the first time the Hollisters heard Scarecrow chuckle. "I'm a distant cousin," he said, "and if I see Santa Claus before next Christmas, I'll tell him to bring an extra big sack of toys to your house." This pleased Sue, who went over and snuggled close to her mother as she gazed into the embers.

For a few minutes after that no one spoke. The fire crackled and the campers listened to the night sounds. Then Mrs. Hollister said, "Scarecrow, who are you?"

The old man stirred, then said slowly, "I know it's not right to keep my identity from you. I'm Professor Nathan Lehigh."

"A professor!" the children chorused.

Scarecrow smiled and unfolded his story. He was a retired college professor and liked the seclusion of the woods. While hiking down the old road one day, he had come upon Fox Lake and the old logging camp. Since it was abandoned he had decided to make his home there.

"Don't you know Mr. Tucker owns it?" Pete asked him.

The old man said he did not know this. "I certainly would have asked permission if I had realized it was private property."

"You didn't scare us when we drove up the road?" Mrs. Hollister asked.

"No, I didn't. But I have an idea who did," he said and told about two men and a boy he had met while wandering in the woods.

"The men laughed and called me 'Scarecrow,' " the professor said, "but the boy seemed afraid to talk."

"I'm sure that was J. B.," said Pam, and told Scarecrow of having met the boy.

The professor agreed that the boy was mysterious and added, "I don't believe those two men are up to any good. I have an idea they may be market hunters."

"Market hunters? What does that mean?" Pam asked.

Scarecrow explained that they were men who hunted game in the woods out of season and sold the meat to big city markets.

"Oh, that's mean!" Holly said indignantly.

"Indeed it is," her father agreed. "Well, Scarecrow, at least part of the mystery is cleared up by learning you're an honest man. Perhaps by the time we finish testing our canoe on Whirlpool River we'll have solved the rest of the riddle."

"I'll help you if I can," the professor said.

"Time for bed, everybody," Mrs. Hollister announced.

Pete picked up a pail and ran to the lake for a bucket with which he doused the fire. He and Ricky decided that Scarecrow should sleep in their tent. They would use their sleeping bags and sleep out under the stars.

When this was agreed upon, the old professor was carried inside the tent. He soon fell fast asleep. But the next morning Scarecrow surprised everyone by limping from his tent unassisted. Using a stick to help him, he hobbled over to Mrs. Hollister who was preparing breakfast.

"It seems as if I'm on the mend," he said. "There's no need for going into town."

"Just the same," Mrs. Hollister declared, smiling, "we're going to take you to the doctor and make sure everything is all right."

"While we're in Glendale," Mr. Hollister said, "we'll pick up more supplies and report the mysterious goings-on of those two men and the boy."

After breakfast Zip was tied to a tree and left to guard the camp. Then everyone stepped into the station wagon and Mr. Hollister headed for the main road. The car jounced along the rutty trail until they came to the place where they had seen the scarecrow.

"Look! It's gone!" Pete exclaimed.

Just then there came a crackling sound. This was followed by a *swoosh* as a huge tree fell across the road directly in front of them!

CHAPTER 10

PORCUPINE QUILLS

"GOODNESS!" Mrs. Hollister cried. "Another few yards and we would have been hit!"

Mr. Hollister drove up to the fallen tree and they all stepped out. There was no one else in sight.

"This must have been done on purpose," Pete declared. "Boy, I'd like to get my hands on——"

"Another note!" Pam cried, as she leapt over the fallen timber.

A piece of a brown paper bag was tacked to the far side of the tree. Pam pulled it off and read to the others:

"Hollisters, when you get to Glendale, keep on going!" It was signed with a skull and crossbones.

Mr. Hollister's face grew red with anger. "Now I'm determined to stay here," he said. "Nobody is going to frighten me out of Spruce Forest!"

His wife smiled at him. "Easy, dear," she said. "With this big tree in front of us it looks as if we'll never get the car out of here."

96

Her good humor relaxed everybody and Pete said, "How are we going to move the tree, Dad? It's too heavy to lift."

Ricky scratched his head and wrinkled his freckled nose. "I have it!" he cried. "We can pull the tree back with our car."

"Excellent idea," said Mr. Hollister. "Did we bring a tow chain, Pete?"

"I put one in the tool compartment."

In a minute Pete had the tow chain and a small saw out. Mr. Hollister sawed through the slender part of the trunk at the edge of the road.

Meanwhile Pete and Ricky attached one end of the chain to the frame of the car. When their father had finished his work, the boys wrapped the other end of the chain around the tree trunk near the cut section. Then Mr. Hollister slid into the driver's seat, put the gear in reverse, and backed up slowly.

Inch by inch the big timber was pulled to the side of the road.

"That does it, Dad!" Pam shouted.

"Ricky, you're a genius," Pete said, patting his brother on the back.

"Sure I am." Ricky grinned.

When the station wagon reached the main road, Mr. Hollister turned left and half an hour later they reached Glendale. They went at once to Doctor Rice's.

The children waited outside while their parents

assisted Professor Lehigh into the office. Fifteen minutes later they returned smiling.

"The professor's leg is not broken, just cut and bruised," Mrs. Hollister said as she helped him into the car.

"Oh, just call me Scarecrow," the old man requested, grinning. "Doc says I'll be all right in a few days."

The physician had given Mr. Hollister directions to the forest ranger's office, which was a small one-story building across the square. They drove there, and the Hollisters went inside.

The State ranger was out ill, so they were referred to Pat Mitchell, the fire warden. He was a tall, good-looking young man dressed in jodhpurs, tunic, and a broad-brimmed hat. He smiled at the children. "What can I do for you?"

"Help us solve a mystery," Holly chirped.

After introductions were made, Mr. Hollister told the story. Pat Mitchell frowned when he heard about the gunshot in the woods.

"No one has a right to be hunting there," he said. "They must be poachers. I'll see to this right away."

"And there was a boy, too," Pete added.

Mitchell, who was jotting down notes, looked up quickly. "Tell me about him," he said.

Pam quickly gave a description and added, "We think his initials are J.B."

Hearing this the warden jumped up from his chair exclaiming, "Jim Blake! You've found him?"

The excited warden told the Hollisters that Jim Blake and his father Roy, a woodsman, had disappeared in the forest two months before. When they had not returned, it was presumed that both had drowned in Whirlpool River because their broken canoe had been found there.

"How dreadful!" said Mrs. Hollister. "But possibly they're alive, and one of those men Pete and Pam saw is Jim's father."

"That's what we'll have to find out," the warden said, and added, "We must tell Mrs. Blake about this clue at once. Follow me."

He strode out the door and went to a small white cottage halfway down the block. When the warden knocked on her door Mrs. Blake answered. She was a short, plump woman with black wavy hair. Her face was haggard with grief. The warden quickly told her what the Hollisters had reported and Mrs. Blake started to cry.

"Are you sure it's my son?" she asked, wringing her hands.

For answer Pam said, "Did he have gray eyes, a straight nose, and hair like yours?"

"Yes, that's my son," the woman said. "And my husband—perhaps he's alive too! If you find my family, I'll be the happiest woman in the world."

"We'll try awful hard," said Sue.

Leaving the Blake home, Pat Mitchell thanked the Hollisters for their information. "I'll go into Spruce

Forest myself," he said, "and track down the illegal hunters."

"If you do," Mr. Hollister said, shaking hands with the warden, "please stop by and see us."

"Thank you."

Mrs. Hollister went to Glendale's general store to buy food. After it had been stowed in the back of the station wagon, the family set off for camp with Scarecrow.

Mr. Hollister drove slowly, fearing another trick by the mysterious men in the woods. But nothing happened.

When he reached the camp site the children jumped out of the car. Pete and Ricky lugged out the boxes of food while the other children raced to greet Zip. A moment later Holly cried out in dismay, "Zip's gone!"

"Did the bad men untie him?" Sue asked.

Pam examined the rope. "It's been cut, or maybe Zip gnawed through it!"

"Maybe he got tired of waiting for us and wanted to romp in the woods," said Holly. She put two fingers into her mouth and whistled for the dog. They all waited anxiously for a few moments, but their pet collie did not appear.

"Oh dear," said Sue, as tears trickled down her cheeks. "Maybe a wild animal got Zip."

Pam put her arm around her small sister and told her not to worry. Zip could take care of himself.

The girls returned to the station wagon and told the others about the missing dog.

Just as Pete and Ricky were about to take off on a hunt for their pet, the sound of howling came from nearby bushes.

"That's Zip!" Pam cried. "Oh, I hope those bad men haven't hurt him."

A moment later the dog bounded into the clearing, shaking his head wildly from side to side.

"Goodness!" Mrs. Hollister exclaimed. "What's the matter with him?"

Scarecrow spoke up. "I think I know," he said. "Here, Zip, come here fellow!"

The dog trotted up to the old man as the children crowded around.

"Just as I thought," Scarecrow said. "Zip tried to get too friendly with a porcupine. See the quills stuck in his nose?"

The professor held the dog's muzzle in his left hand and plucked out the small quills.

"You mean a porcupine shot him?" Ricky asked.

"No, not at all," Scarecrow said with a chuckle. "Porky is a shy, retiring animal and doesn't shoot his quills as some tenderfoot woodsmen believe."

Pam patted the dog who now seemed much relieved. "Did Zip nudge the porcupine with his nose, Scarecrow?" she asked.

"That's what he must have done," the man replied, and added with a smile, "I'll guarantee that Zip won't get so curious about Mr. Porky next time."

"Tell us more about Mr. Porky," Sue requested.

Scarecrow sat down on a stump. "They love salt," he said, "and frequently prowl around a camp to find some. And do you know what they sometimes eat?"

"Saltines!" Sue chirped.

The old man nodded. "And anything with salt on it—even ax handles."

"Really?" Pam asked.

Scarecrow said that ax handles get salt on them from people's moist palms and sometimes porcupines chew on them. Holly glanced at their own ax which lay embedded in a stump nearby. She ran over to examine it. A few tiny teeth marks were scratched on the handle.

"Porky was trying to eat our ax!" she cried, patting the collie's head. "And Zip chased him away, trying to protect the camp!"

Zip liked the praise he received and trotted about wagging his tail.

That evening the sun was a huge red ball as it set over the treetops in Spruce Forest. As the Hollisters and Scarecrow watched it, the children's father said, "I'll test my canoe tomorrow in Whirlpool River if the weather is good."

"The rapids are dangerous," Scarecrow warned him. "Are you an experienced canoeist?"

Mr. Hollister said that he had handled canoes for many years and thought he could negotiate the white water of Whirlpool River. "I'll take Pete and Ricky with me."

"That's keen," said Ricky.

Scarecrow glanced at the last sliver of sun as it disappeared. "I think it'll be a fine day tomorrow," he remarked. "There's an old woodsman's saying that goes:

Evening red, morning gray
Sets the traveler on his way;
Evening gray, morning red
Brings down the rain upon his head!"

"Well," Mrs. Hollister said, "the evening certainly is red. If it's gray tomorrow morning that will mean a fine day."

As they sat around the campfire later, Scarecrow said, "There are dangerous rapids at three points in Whirlpool River. If your collapsible canoe gets through safely, I'd say your invention is a success, Mr. Hollister."

The professor mapped out the river route, pointing out the danger spots. "And here's a portage you can take back," he said. "Just follow the old blaze marks which start here at the big rock." He penciled the spot on the map.

Pete and Ricky were excited about the trip. The older boy was to take the bow paddle while Ricky would sit in the bottom of the canoe with their packs.

"Jiminy, I wish we girls could go," Holly said, disappointed.

"Me, too," said Pam.

When Sue declared that she also would like to see the "white rabbits," everyone chuckled. Pam explained to her they were talking about rapids.

Mrs. Hollister said, "We'll find something for you girls to do."

"Of course we will," Scarecrow said. "As a matter of fact I'll show you how to make beans-in-a-hole."

"What's that?" Holly asked.

"I'll show you tomorrow," Scarecrow said with a wink. "It's a delicious dish and should be ready for the canoeists by the time they return tomorrow night."

The old man insisted on sleeping outdoors so as not to deprive the boys of their tent. The Hollisters made him a comfortable bed beside the campfire. As the children said goodnight, they saw Zip snuggle up beside Scarecrow.

Before sunup the next morning Pete and Ricky were roused by their father. "Come on, boys," he said softly, shaking them to wakefulness. "We'll start on our trip as soon as possible."

The three girls were still asleep, but Mrs. Hollister and Scarecrow were already preparing breakfast. Wisps of fog drifted from the glassy surface of Fox Lake. The sky was gray.

"If the old weather prophets were correct," Mrs. Hollister said, smiling, "you canoeists should have a good day."

After breakfast she kissed her sons and husband,

then Pete launched the canoe, stepping in to man the front paddle. Ricky flung the knapsacks in the bottom and sat happily among them while his father shoved off. In a few seconds they had disappeared into the haze on Fox Lake.

Following the directions which Scarecrow had given them, Mr. Hollister made a beeline toward the forepaw of the fox. This was where the water spilled out of the lake into Whirlpool River.

He and the boys reached the place in half an hour. When the sound of the roaring water greeted their ears, Mr. Hollister said, "Hold on tight, boys. Here we go!"

The canoe bounced and lurched in the foaming water as he guided it expertly between the rocks.

Suddenly Ricky shouted, "Look out, Pete!"

A large boulder loomed up ahead. Pete reached out with his paddle and pushed against it. The canoe darted past, inches from the jagged obstruction.

"Good work, Pete," Mr. Hollister called out as they continued through the rapids. Then he added, "Let me know when you see the whirlpool."

"There's one up ahead," Pete reported.

As Scarecrow had instructed him, Mr. Hollister veered far to the right side of the river while making the canoe glide at the edge of the churning water. Suddenly the paddlers found themselves in a calm stretch of the river.

"Hurray! We made the first rapids!" Ricky shouted.

"Look out, Pete!"

"How's the canoe?" Mr. Hollister asked his son.

"Tight, Dad!" Ricky said proudly. "Every seam held."

Although the water was calm, the current was swift. Mr. Hollister had little to do except guide the craft down the beautiful stream. By now the sun was shining low in the eastern sky, its rays dancing off the droplets on the flashing paddles.

Mr. Hollister reached into the pocket for the map which Scarecrow had made. He handed it over to Ricky. "You be the navigator, son. Where do we hit the second rapids?"

Ricky studied the map. "After the next bend in the river, Dad."

Ten minutes later they came to the place where the river turned left. Before them they could see white water again.

"We approach this one from the right side," Mr. Hollister said. "All set, Pete?"

"Right, skipper."

Soon the foamy water slapped at the bottom of the canoe. The craft lurched as it slid through the second rapids.

Suddenly Pete called out, "Brace yourselves!"

Before them a cable was stretched across the rapids a few inches above water level. The front of the canoe hit it and slewed around.

"Hang on!" Mr. Hollister called, bending low to balance the canoe.

But the craft was out of control. It scraped over the wire and turned about broadside in the raging stream. A second later it hit a rock and flipped over.

Mr. Hollister and his two sons were thrown into Whirlpool River!

CHAPTER 11

THE RESCUE

"GRAB the canoe!" Mr. Hollister cried out as the three were swept downstream with the overturned craft.

Pete reached up through the milky water and grabbed the bow of the canoe as it slipped past.

His father, meanwhile, swam about looking for Ricky, who was not in sight. In a moment Pete saw him. "Ricky's downstream!" he shouted.

The boy had bobbed to the surface, but he was floating face down, moving his arms feebly.

"He's been stunned!" Mr. Hollister cried as he swam toward the lad with powerful strokes. But the current was so strong that Ricky was carried along nearly as fast as his father could swim.

Just then Pete spotted a dark-haired boy on the river bank below them. The lad kicked off his moccasins, raced into the swirling eddies, and swam directly toward Ricky.

Before Mr. Hollister could reach the spot, the boy flipped Ricky over on his back and towed him to shore. Then, slipping into his moccasins again, he dashed off into the woods.

"I wonder if that was J. B.," Mr. Hollister asked himself as he splashed up to the river bank. Immediately he applied artificial respiration to his son, while Pete dragged the canoe and packs ashore.

"Dad, is he all right?" Pete asked, worried.

As Mr. Hollister nodded, Ricky groaned and his eyelids flickered open. In a few minutes he had regained his breath and sat up.

"Thanks for saving me, Dad."

"I'm not the hero," Mr. Hollister said.

"No, it was J. B.," Pete said. "I recognized him as he ran off. Do you suppose he had anything to do with stretching the cable across the river?"

"I doubt it," his father replied. "I believe that men who have no business in the forest are trying to make it as dangerous as possible for anybody to camp here."

Jim Blake, they agreed, was perhaps the biggest mystery of all. Why had he warned them to leave, and now rescued Ricky but fled at once? What was he trying to hide? And where was his father?

The Hollisters sat in the sun on the river bank drying out themselves and their packs. Then they collapsed the canoe, hid their gear in a clump of bushes, and scoured the area in search of Jim Blake.

For a while the boys and their father followed his footprints in the soft earth of the river bank. But once in rocky terrain they lost track of the lad's trail completely.

"I think," said Mr. Hollister, "that we've given

our canoe a real test. Now we'd better try to pick up the old portage, get back to camp as quickly as possible, and report this river cable."

"First, let me examine it," Pete requested.

He found that the heavy steel wire was attached to a bolt imbedded in the rock.

"I'd cut it now if I could," Mr. Hollister said, "but we haven't the proper tools."

The Hollisters shouldered their packs. Then with Mr. Hollister toting the collapsed canoe, they set off at right angles from the river in search of the old portage trail.

The map which Ricky had held had been washed overboard, but his father recalled that the trail paralleled the river. Walking cautiously through the deep brush, the three made their way slowly through the forest. Every tree was examined for traces of old blaze marks.

"We must have missed the trail!" Ricky said after a while. "I think we're lost."

Mr. Hollister looked at his pocket compass. They were headed due west in the right direction.

"Let's push on a little farther," Pete said.

Hitching their packs higher on their shoulders, the three travelers pressed ahead. Pete carefully examined a big fir tree.

"Look here!" he cried out. "I've found an old blaze mark!"

Mr. Hollister and Ricky hurried to his side. "This

111

is the one all right," said his father. "No doubt about it."

Ricky dashed on ahead, going north by his compass. "And here's another one!" he shouted. "We're on our way!"

Before proceeding farther, however, Mr. Hollister ordered his sons to throw down their packs. "A little chow will help us," he said.

Pete broke open a tin of corned beef while Ricky unrolled a loaf of bread from an oilskin wrapper. The boys made sandwiches while their father poured hot chocolate from a thermos.

"Um! This is delicious," Ricky said as he nibbled the last crumb of his sandwich.

Greatly refreshed, the Hollisters flung their packs on again and followed the old blaze marks. Half an hour later they came to a huge boulder.

"Crickets! It's as high as a house," Pete observed.

As the three stopped to gaze up at the mass of rock, they heard the cracking of a twig.

"What was that?" Ricky whispered.

"I think someone's on the other side of the rock," his father said.

"Poachers?" Pete wondered.

"Perhaps."

"Let's try to capture them, Dad," Ricky said, making a fist. "After what they did to us!"

Mr. Hollister advised caution. "First, we'll have to scout them," he said, "and see what they're up to."

"I'll do it," Pete volunteered.

"All right, but be quiet and careful," his father said.

Pete took off his knapsack and moved silently around the base of the rock, tiptoeing so as not to disturb the slightest twig.

Five minutes later he was back walking as stealthily as an Indian on a scouting mission. "Dad!" he whispered hoarsely, "there's only one man. He's examining a heap of animal skins."

"Did you get a good look at him?" Mr. Hollister asked.

"No. Only his back. He's wearing a plaid flannel shirt."

Mr. Hollister decided they must act at once. "Pete and Ricky, you creep around the left side of the rock. I'll go in the other direction. We'll converge on the poacher and take him by surprise."

Leaving their packs behind the huge boulder, the three set off silently. After inching along carefully Pete and Ricky came near the man. He was still bending over the animal skins. In a moment the boys' father flanked them on the right side.

Mr. Hollister stood up and gave a sign to his sons. "Attack!" he yelled.

The three dashed forward and before the stranger could turn about in surprise they flung themselves at him. Rolling over and over on the ground Mr. Hollister got a headlock on the man while the boys grabbed his feet.

Suddenly the man cried out. "Let me go, Mr. Hollister!"

The boys' father looked into the man's face. "Good night!" he cried out. "Pat Mitchell!"

They all rose from the ground and the Hollisters apologized.

The fire warden grinned ruefully. "I thought I was being attacked by a pack of wild Indians. Who did you think I was?"

"The poacher!" Ricky cried.

"Well, a poacher was here. I arrived too late to catch him." The warden pointed to the skins on the ground. "Several deer were killed and butchered on the spot. Probably for easier portage by the market hunters," he said. "Now I know what's been going on in Spruce Forest."

"You don't suppose Roy Blake is involved in this, do you?" Mr. Hollister asked.

"That has me baffled," Mitchell admitted. "I've always thought Blake was a fine fellow."

"We saw Jim again," Pete said, and told how Ricky had been pulled from the raging stream.

"Well, the mystery certainly gets deeper," the warden said, picking up the hunting cap he had been wearing.

"Listen!" Ricky cried out, as a gun shot sounded from deep in the forest.

"The poachers!" Pat Mitchell exclaimed. He dashed off among the trees.

"We'll help you!" Pete offered.

114

"*Attack!*"

The warden stopped. "I can do this better alone," he said. "It's dangerous because they're armed. I wouldn't want you to get hurt."

"Okay, we'll go back," Mr. Hollister said. "Good luck to you!"

After picking up their packs, the three hikers followed the portage trail toward camp.

"I wonder what the girls are doing right now," Pete mused.

At that very moment Pam, Holly, and Sue were talking with Scarecrow. "Please show us how to make beans-in-the-hole," Holly begged.

"All right," the old man said. "But first we must decide who will be the cooks and who will be the fire tenders."

Holly spoke up. "I'll be a fire tender."

"And I'll help you," said Sue, who was holding a doll she had brought along.

It was decided that Pam and Mrs. Hollister would prepare the ingredients. Scarecrow told them to boil two quarts of beans until the skins wrinkled, then cover the bottom of a large pot with slices of onion.

"Dump enough of the drained beans in to fill half the bean pot," he instructed. "Now add another layer of onions, with large slabs of salt pork on top of the onions."

Pam smiled. "And then pour in the rest of the beans?"

"Correct! Also, add a cup of molasses," Scarecrow said. He turned to Holly and Sue. "You little

116

chipmunks, dig a hole large enough to hold the pot. Gather twigs and wood to start a fire directly over the hole."

Sue dashed off to get the wood while Holly went for a shovel. She dug a hole some little distance away. When it was deep enough, Scarecrow lighted the twigs and soon a merry fire was burning over the pit.

"Just keep putting twigs on it, Holly," he said and walked off.

Sue stood by watching the fire. She held her doll by one hand, its dress dragging on the ground.

All at once Pam, walking toward her, cried out, "Sue! Your doll's on fire!"

CHAPTER 12

WHITECAP TROUBLE

"OH, MY poor baby!" Sue cried out, seeing the smoke curl up from the skirt of her doll's dress.

In two great leaps Pam jumped to her sister's side. Grabbing the doll, she raced to the water's edge and dipped the blazing toy.

Szzt! The fire went out instantly. The excitement brought Mrs. Hollister and Scarecrow to the scene.

"Good for you, Pam," her mother said. "That was quick thinking."

"Oh thank you, Pam," said Sue. She examined the doll and found that only the dress had been ruined. "I'll get her another one."

Holly, under the watchful eyes of Scarecrow, piled more wood onto the fire. As the burning sticks turned to glowing coals, they fell to the bottom of the hole.

"Fine! That's just what we want," the old man said.

By the time the beans were ready in the pot, the hole was full of hot embers. Scarecrow took the pot, made sure the lid was fastened securely, and carefully placed it in the hole.

"Next we cover everything over with the earth Holly dug," Scarecrow said.

Holly took her shovel and mounded the dirt over the pot of beans. "Now what?" she asked.

"That's all there is to do," Scarecrow said, smiling. "We'll let it cook slowly all day, and tonight when your daddy and the boys return we'll have a real feast."

The sun was high and the day hot. "Perfect weather for swimming," Mrs. Hollister said. "Let's all take a dip."

The three girls scrambled into their tent and put on their swim suits. Mrs. Hollister joined them a few moments later.

"One, two, three! Go!" Holly cried out, and was first into the water.

All the Hollisters were excellent swimmers with the exception of Sue. Whenever she went into the water she wore a bright-orange life jacket.

As Scarecrow watched from a camp chair near the edge of the lake, Mrs. Hollister and the three girls swam about. Presently Holly came out and got a big blue plastic ball from her tent. She tossed it far out in the water. Pam went after it.

"Let's play a game," Holly said.

They tossed the ball to one another. Each miss counted one point against the loser. The game was so spirited that the players did not notice Scarecrow quietly leave his seat, pick up Pete's hatchet, and disappear into the woods.

119

"Watch this one," cried Holly. She made a fist and bounced the ball high into the air.

Plop! It came down on Sue's head and bounced onto the shore. It was then that the Hollisters noticed Scarecrow was missing.

"Where did he go?" Pam called out as she climbed from the water.

"Scarecrow! Scarecrow! Where are you?" Sue shouted.

The professor did not appear, but they could hear the sound of wood being chopped. Shortly afterward Scarecrow emerged, carrying a slender six-foot log under each arm.

"Are you going to build a log house?" Holly asked him.

The old man grinned. "Something you'll like better than that. Wait here while I get the rest of the timbers."

He made several trips into the woods, bringing out six more poles and an armful of trailing vines.

Pam's eyes sparkled. "Are you going to build a raft, Scarecrow?"

"That's right," he said with a chuckle, "and you girls and your mother can help me."

The old man showed the girls how to lash the logs together near the water's edge and in half an hour the float was ready.

"That's neat!" Pam said in delight.

"We can dive off it, can't we?" Holly remarked, clapping her hands.

With a splash they launched the homemade float. Pam and Holly pushed it out into the water with one hand, paddling with the other and kicking their feet. Then the two girls climbed aboard.

"Thank you so much, Mr. Lehigh," the children's mother said. "It certainly is a wonderful plaything."

"I want to get on too," Sue said as she splashed and bobbed about, trying to reach the float.

Mrs. Hollister pushed Sue to the edge of the raft and Pam pulled her onto it. The little girl stood up and shielded the sun from her eyes as she gazed far out over the lake.

"I'm a dangerous pirate!" she cried out, and the others laughed.

"I wish Pete and Ricky could see us," Holly called out, as she kicked her feet in the water over the side of the raft. "They—oh ouch! A crab's got me!"

Holly pulled up one foot. With it came Pam, who had swum under the raft and tickled Holly's toes.

"Oh, you meanie!" Holly said, giggling.

Sue was content to sit in the middle of the raft and look around. Suddenly, while she was gazing toward shore, a strange-looking creature stuck its head out of the water.

"Mother! What is it?" Sue cried, scrambling to her feet. The head disappeared, but returned a few seconds later. "Will it hurt us?" she asked, worried.

Mrs. Hollister chuckled. "No. That's a little otter," she said. "Let's see where it goes."

The animal, startled by the splashing of the Hollisters, swam toward shore. Then, pulling itself along on its webbed, clawed feet, the otter sat down atop a little muddy mound on the water front.

The Hollisters watched, fascinated, as two more otters appeared on the surface of the water. They joined the other animal on the mud mound. Then, to the children's delight, all three slid down into the water.

"They're playing a game!" Sue cried out joyfully.

"I want to get a better look," said Holly as she slipped off the raft and swam toward shore.

Meanwhile Pam and her mother pushed the raft until it touched the bank a little distance from the otters' playground. They stepped ashore, but Sue decided to stay aboard and watch the otters from there.

Holly had run to tell Scarecrow about the otters and he hobbled back to the spot with her.

"Don't go too close to them," the professor said, "or they'll dive down into their underwater home."

Quietly the group tiptoed along the beach for a better view.

"Otters are curious little fellows," Scarecrow said, and chuckled when Pam remarked that they looked like sea dragons.

"Yes. And they love to slide," the old man went on. He added that they slid on snow in the winter and mud in the summer.

"Oh look!" Holly exclaimed. "Aren't they cute!"

At that moment one of the otters stood on top of the mud slide awaiting his turn to go down. His playmate, directly behind, pushed him off and went down himself. The two tussled with each other as they splashed into the water.

Holly said, smiling, "Even the forest children like to play games, don't they?"

Her mother nodded in agreement and turned her head for a moment to look at Sue. The little girl was stretched out over the edge of the raft paddling with her hands and pushing the float out from shore.

"Come back, Sue!" her mother called.

At this moment a black wind cloud obscured the sun and a breeze sprang up. It blew from the land, and pushed the raft before it.

"Oh dear!" Mrs. Hollister said.

She dived into the water, and swam as fast as she could toward the runaway float. Pam and Holly followed.

Sue did not realize what had happened. Now she stood up, looking across the water. This made her body act as a sail and the raft moved even more swiftly out into the lake. Little whitecaps began to kick up the surface.

Mrs. Hollister called out, "Sue, lie face down on the raft. Don't move about!"

But the wind was too strong for her voice to carry to the little girl.

Holly and Pam looked in fright at their mother.

"Come back, Sue!"

"We'll never catch her," Holly declared, her wet pigtails streaming along behind her.

Mrs. Hollister paused long enough to instruct her daughters. "Both of you swim back to shore and see if Daddy is back yet," she said. "I'll continue after Sue."

Reluctantly Pam and Holly turned back while Mrs. Hollister, with a determined look on her face, increased the speed of her strokes. Sue was unconcerned, thinking this was some sort of game. She danced about on the raft, clapping her hands. "Mother, you can't catch me!"

Mrs. Hollister felt herself tiring. In alarm she realized she must reach the raft in the next few minutes or give up hope of rescuing her small daughter. Putting on an extra burst of speed, her arms cut through the choppy waters.

Finally, with a lunge, her right hand touched the float and she held on. Getting her breath, Mrs. Hollister pulled herself up beside Sue. By now the lake shore looked far away.

"How am I going to get back?" she wondered.

Sue, giggling disappointedly, "Oh Mother, you caught me!"

"It's a good thing I did," Mrs. Hollister replied, panting for breath. "Please don't go on a runaway raft again."

Seeing the worried look on her mother's face, Sue promised. Then a little timidly she asked, "Can you get us back, Mommy?"

"I'll try." Mrs. Hollister lowered herself into the water and grasping the raft on the leeward side, kicked her feet hard. But she could make no headway in the face of the strong wind.

Climbing aboard again, she gazed back toward the shore. She could faintly make out Pam and Holly waving white handkerchiefs.

Squinting her eyes, Mrs. Hollister saw them pointing to the south end of the big lake. She looked in that direction. Was it a canoe they were waving at and who was in it?

CHAPTER 13

FRIEND OR FOE

THERE was a tense wait as the canoe approached, then Mrs. Hollister said in relief, "Daddy and the boys are coming!"

She and Sue waved their arms to attract the attention of the paddlers.

"They've seen us!" Mrs. Hollister cried as the canoe turned in their direction.

It came quickly, bouncing over the whitecaps. When Mr. Hollister was within hailing distance, he called out:

"Hold tight! We'll get you!"

As the canoe pulled alongside, Ricky reached out and grasped the raft.

"Are you all right?" Mr. Hollister asked, helping his wife and daughter to step into the canoe. They assured him they were.

The boys admired the raft and wanted to take it along, so the float was tied to the stern of the canoe. Then the paddlers started for camp.

Sue, who sat facing her father, said, "We had lots of fun today. Did you?"

127

"It was very exciting," Mr. Hollister said, and told what had happened.

"J. B. sure is brave," said Ricky. "I wish we could find him and take him back to his mother."

"We'll certainly do our best," his father replied.

When they reached the lake edge, Pam, Holly, and Scarecrow helped them ashore.

As the wind whipped their faces, Mr. Hollister remarked, "This is quite a blow!"

"We may have a real storm later tonight," Scarecrow said.

"Then we'd better have supper early," Mrs. Hollister remarked.

"We're having beans-in-the-hole," Pam announced. "Is it ready, Scarecrow?"

The professor nodded and motioned Holly to get her shovel. Carefully the girl cleared the dirt from the top of the pit. Scarecrow picked up a pair of pot holders and lifted the red-hot container out of the coals. As he removed the lid, the steaming aroma of the baked beans and pork made everyone's mouth water.

"Boy, what a feast!" Pete said in delight.

Plates were filled with the delicious food and passed around by Pam. Presently Zip nudged Holly, and she set a little portion of the meat on a paper plate. Then she added dog biscuits and poured some of the juice over them. He finished the food before the Hollisters had eaten half of theirs!

After the supper had been cleared away, Scarecrow said, "I must be getting back to my hut. Thanks for everything you nice people have done for me."

"You can't go now!" Mrs. Hollister protested. "You still have a slight limp and the storm may get worse before you reach there."

The old man waved a weather-beaten hand. "Don't worry about me," he said. "I'm used to the woods. Besides, I've been your guest long enough. I must leave you now."

When he could not be persuaded to stay, Mr. Hollister went for a handful of trail blazes. "Take these with you in case you need them."

The old woodsman took the handful and stuffed them into a trouser pocket. "Well, good-by and thanks again."

The Hollisters were sorry to see the old professor depart. They felt a little sense of alarm as the man limped off along the trail with the wind blowing through his white whiskers.

"Oh dear, I hope he makes it all right," Pam said when he had disappeared from sight.

Before bedtime Pete and his father collapsed the canoe and stowed it with some other equipment under one of the trees. By the time everyone had retired, the wind's howling grew even louder.

The Hollisters fell asleep worrying about Scarecrow, and Ricky dreamed the man was in the roaring rapids. The noise of the churning water had reached a deafening crescendo when Ricky sud-

"The tent pegs are coming loose!"

denly awoke. The noise he had heard was the storm outside, now at its peak.

Pete too had awakened and flashed on his light. The walls of their tent were swaying first one way, then the other.

"Pete! It's going to blow down on us!" Ricky cried in alarm.

"I think the tent pegs are coming loose," Pete said. "We'll have to drive them deeper in the ground!"

Quickly putting on their slickers the boys grabbed their hatchets and ran out into the windstorm. They saw a flashlight bobbing in front of their father's tent.

"Dad, is that you?" Ricky called out.

"Yes. The tent pegs are coming loose."

"Ours, too," Pete replied, and the brothers began to drive them deeper. They did the same for their sisters' tent.

Suddenly a flash of lightning made the forest as bright as day. It was followed by the crashing sounds of thunder. Almost instantly rain came down in a torrent.

"Yikes! That was close!" Ricky observed.

The three Hollisters ducked back into their tents.

The rain beat down like a thousand fingers drumming on the waterproof canvas. The wind abated and the boys were lulled to sleep by the steady downpour.

Some time later the storm ended. When the family awakened next morning, the sun was up over the ridge of hills. Zip poked his nose out of the girls' tent and busied himself looking for frogs while the Hollisters prepared breakfast.

"I do hope Mr. Lehigh made it back to his hut safely," Mrs. Hollister remarked as she slipped a sunnyside-up egg onto Holly's metal plate.

"I do too," Pam declared. "Scarecrow certainly is a kind old man."

As the family finished their bacon and eggs, Zip started to bark loudly.

Pam chuckled. "A big bull frog must be bothering him," she said.

"It's not that," Ricky burst out. "Someone's coming to our camp."

All eyes turned to see a uniformed man striding toward them from among the trees. He wore green trousers and tunic and the sleeves were too long for his short arms. The stranger was hatless and as he approached, Pam noticed he had bushy eyebrows and a thin tight mouth.

"I'm Henry Sharp, one of the forest rangers," he said, introducing himself.

"And we're the Hollisters," the children's father said. "My name is John."

"Yes, I know all about you," Mr. Sharp said. "That's why I'm here."

Mrs. Hollister looked uneasy. "Is something wrong?" she asked.

132

"Yes, there is," the ranger said gruffly. "I came upon a lobstick in the woods early this morning. It had a note on it that you Hollisters have been mistreating the forest animals."

"Oh no," said Pam. "That's not true."

The ranger glanced at her out of the corner of his eyes. "Then what did you do?" he asked.

Mrs. Hollister supplied the answer, telling how they had rescued an injured fawn. "It was returned to its doe," she said, "and my children certainly treated it kindly."

"Wait a minute," Mr. Hollister said. "Who is this person who complained about us?"

The ranger fingered the cuffs of his long sleeves. "It was signed Scarecrow," he said. "He gets around these woods and knows a lot."

"Scarecrow!" the children cried out in unison.

"He's our friend," Pete said defiantly. "He wouldn't complain about us."

Mr. Hollister stepped up to the man. "We don't like to doubt your word," he said, "but may I see your credentials?"

The man pulled a wallet from his pocket and displayed a card which stated that Henry Sharp was a forest ranger. Then with a smile that was more like a sneer he said:

"I'm sorry but I'll have to order you out of these woods."

"You can't do that!" Mr. Hollister said firmly.

"We're guests of Mr. Tucker, who owns this place."

"That makes no difference," the ranger replied.

"But suppose we can prove our innocence," Pam pleaded. "I'm certain that Scarecrow didn't write that message."

Mr. Sharp shrugged his shoulders. "Well, if you can prove it, I might let you stay."

"By the way," Mr. Hollister said, "someone gave us a bad time in the rapids yesterday. Do you know there's a cable stretched across Whirlpool River?"

The ranger looked surprised and when Mr. Hollister told him where the obstruction was located, Sharp said he would attend to it.

"I'll be back tomorrow for your answer," he said. "I hope you find Scarecrow to prove your point."

With that he turned and stalked off into the forest. Sue burst into tears. "I thought Scarecrow was such a nice man!" she wailed.

"I believe he is," said Mr. Hollister, "and he wouldn't complain about us. Someone else may have used his name on the lobstick."

The other Hollisters were of the same opinion and Pete brought up a new idea. "I think that ranger is a phony. Maybe he stole those identification papers."

Pam's eyes lighted up. "Then maybe the story about Scarecrow's note isn't true either."

Mrs. Hollister warned that they should not accuse anybody without proof of guilt, then she added,

"Let's go straight to Scarecrow and ask for an explanation."

Pam helped her mother pack a lunch and soon the family was ready for the trail. Zip had disappeared into the woods, and though the boys called and whistled their pet did not appear.

Pete thought he heard faint barking. "I'll find Zip," he said. "You go ahead. I'll catch up with you."

The other children wanted to search too. Mrs. Hollister finally gave her consent for all except Sue to accompany Pete. "Don't go far," she said. "We'll wait here."

Ricky and Pete kept whistling for the dog. Presently they heard barking which sounded like Zip's, but repeated calls failed to bring him to their side.

"Something's wrong, Pete," Pam said nervously. "I'm sure Zip heard us."

Following the sounds of the dog's barks, the children crashed through the undergrowth.

"We ought to make blaze marks," Pam warned.

"There's no time for that!" Holly cried impatiently. "Zip may be in trouble." She and Ricky sprinted ahead.

"Come back! Don't get too far ahead of us!" Pam cried out.

In a moment she and Pete caught up with the other children and Holly said, "Listen! Zip's barks are louder now!"

135

Pressing on through the dense woods Pete suddenly saw an odd mark on one of the trees.

"A fresh blaze mark!" he told Pam. "Someone's been pretty close to our camp and——"

Suddenly two rough-looking men leaped out from behind a big spruce tree with Zip barking at their heels.

CHAPTER 14

A TELLTALE KNIFE

STARTLED by the two men, the Hollister children stopped and stared. The taller of the men spoke first. "If this is your dog, get him away!" he said, scowling.

Pam called her pet, and he ran to her side, his ears flattened against his head.

Pete asked, "Who are you?"

"We're surveyors," the shorter man said. "Keep your dog tied. We don't want him around."

The other fellow spoke up. "These woods are dangerous for children. I'd advise you to get out of here."

Suddenly Pete's eyes widened in surprise as he stared at the taller man, but he said nothing.

"All right," Pam agreed politely. "We'll tell our parents what you said. But what are these dangers?"

"If you don't leave, you'll find out soon enough," the smaller man said. With that the two strode away. Zip wanted to chase them but Pam held onto his collar.

When the two men were out of sight, Pete grasped his sister's arm. "Pam," he said, "did you see what that tall fellow had attached to his belt?"

"No, what?"

"A Geiger counter!" Pete declared. "The same kind that was stolen from our store."

"You mean he's one of the thieves?" Pam gasped.

"I think we'd better find out," Pete answered. "Let's tell Mother and Dad right away."

The four children retraced their steps toward the spot where the others waited. Mr. Hollister, seeing them, started along the trail at a brisk pace.

"Wait for us!" Pete called. "We have something to tell you!"

Scrambling up the hill the four children reached Mr. and Mrs. Hollister and quickly told their story.

"This is mighty serious," their father said, frowning. "Those fellows are hunting for uranium on private property without permission from Mr. Tucker."

"Oh dear," Mrs. Hollister said. "They could be the market hunters that Pat Mitchell is looking for. We must tell him."

"And also ask Mr. Mitchell if he knows the forest ranger Sharp," Pete said.

"But first we ought to see if Scarecrow is all right," Mrs. Hollister said.

"Yes, we should," her husband agreed.

They hurried along the trail and soon the old sawmill came into view. Pete and Pam raced ahead. When they reached the front of the old, tumble-down bunkhouse, Pam stopped short.

"Look, Pete!" she said, pointing to the ground.

The tall grass had been trampled and several bushes were broken. Pete ran to the door.

"Scarecrow!" he cried out. "Scarecrow, where are you?"

The hut was empty!

The Hollisters searched the place thoroughly but there was no sign of Scarecrow. Pam said, "I think he was kidnaped."

The signs of the scuffle outside the cabin door led her parents to believe this might be true.

"Those two surveyors may have been here," Pete said.

"I'll report all this to the police immediately," his father replied.

"And check on Sharp, the ranger," Pam reminded him.

Ricky, with the aid of Zip, had found three sets of footprints and the Hollisters followed the tracks. They led to the lake shore and ended there.

Pam looked worried and said, "Poor Scarecrow was probably carried off in a canoe."

She and the others scanned the lake for sight of a craft, but all they could see was a blue heron skimming over the surface of the still water.

"Let's eat lunch and then hurry back to camp," Mr. Hollister said.

The food was brought out. After the Hollisters had eaten it, they started along the trail.

Looking carefully about as they trudged along, the family saw nothing suspicious. Half a mile from camp, however, a clear warbling whistle arrested their attention.

"That sounds like a cardinal," Mrs. Hollister remarked.

Pete listened carefully, then shook his head. "I think it's someone whistling, Mother. And not far away."

"Let's investigate!" Ricky said excitedly.

"Go ahead," his father agreed, "but take Zip along with you."

The two boys and the dog headed into the direction of the whistling. It seemed to come from a clump of birch trees in a hollow. Reaching the place, they looked about. The whistling had stopped.

"I guess Mr. Bird flew away," Ricky said.

Zip nosed about in the brush, suddenly flushing a grouse which whirred off among the trees. The dog bounded off in hot pursuit of the bird, with Ricky following close behind. Pete stood still. A moment later the warbling sounded again, this time from behind a huge fallen oak tree. As Pete stepped toward it a black-haired boy sprang up.

"J.B.!" Pete cried.

"Not so loud," the other boy replied in a hoarse whisper. "They might hear us!"

"Who might?"

"I can't tell you now," J.B. said, his eyes darting about furtively. "But they're following every move you make in the woods."

Pete took a step forward, beckoning to the strange boy to come closer. "Please tell us what this mystery is all about," he begged. "If you're in trouble, maybe we can help you. Trust me!"

J.B. looked to the ground and shook his head. "You can't help me," he said and his voice sounded forlorn. "Thanks anyway."

"But are you Jim Blake? If you are, your mother is terribly worried. And where is your father?"

Startled, the boy looked up. "I promised not to——please leave Spruce Forest," he said pleadingly. Then he added, "But if you do get into trouble you'll find a sign two hundred paces west of your camp."

Pete puzzled over this a moment and went on hurriedly. "If you'll only tell my Dad all about yourself I'm sure he can help you," he persisted. "Come with me now."

"I can't. I mustn't!"

Suddenly Pete thought of a bold plan. If he could only grab the boy, hold onto him, and call the other Hollisters! If this was Jim Blake, it was Pete's duty to bring him home to his mother—no matter what!

"They're following every move you make."

Springing forward over the log, Pete wrestled J.B. to the ground, at the same time crying out:

"Dad, I have him! Help!"

"Let me go!" J.B. yelled as they rolled over and over.

The mysterious boy was considerably stronger than Pete and managed to break out of the bear hold which Pete had clamped about him.

As J.B. struggled to his feet he could hear the other Hollisters crashing through the woods toward him. In desperation he thrust his hands under Pete's chin. Then with a strong push he sent his opponent toppling backward over the fallen log.

"Pete, where are you?" cried Mr. Hollister as he led the others through the dense growth.

"Here I am!" Pete called. "Come quickly!"

J.B. turned with a frightened look and raced off.

"What happened?" Mr. Hollister asked as he came upon his son picking himself up from the ground. Just then Ricky and Zip returned after an unsuccessful pursuit of the grouse.

"I almost had J.B.!" Pete said, disappointedly. "But he got away."

After Pete had told the entire story of the encounter, Pam remarked, "Somebody is threatening poor Jim Blake—if it really is Jim."

Sue bent down behind the stump and picked up a pocket knife. "Is this yours, Pete?" she asked.

"No, it isn't. I'll bet J.B. dropped it."

As the others crowded about him, Pete examined the knife. Pulling out a shiny blade he said, "Crickets, look at this!" On it was inscribed: "J.B. from Dad."

"Now we can find out if this boy really is Jim Blake," Mr. Hollister said. "We'll take this knife to town and show it to Mrs. Blake."

"Come on! Let's go," Ricky urged.

Pete caught up with his brother and together they kept up a steady trot until they came within sight of their camp. Suddenly the boys stopped short.

"Yikes! Look what's happened!" Ricky yelled. "Our tents are gone! Mother, Dad! Hurry!"

Zip raced on ahead barking furiously and sniffing about the camp site. Mr. Hollister caught up to his sons and they dashed into the clearing as the others followed.

"Our camp's been ransacked" Mr. Hollister exclaimed in alarm.

Not only were the tents missing but so were their supplies which had been piled beneath a tarpaulin under one of the spruce trees. The only things left were the family's swim suits strung on a rope between two trees at the edge of the camp site.

"Dad! The canoe was stolen too!" Holly sobbed.

Mrs. Hollister glanced across the clearing where they had left their station wagon. "Thank goodness our car is still here!" she said.

Mr. Hollister's face was grave. "We'll drive to town and report this!"

As his family dashed toward the car, they again cried out in dismay.

All four tires had been taken off! Even the spare was missing!

CHAPTER 15

A DANGEROUS SHORTCUT

"THOSE mean thieves!" Holly said hotly. "What will we do now?"

Ricky looked appealingly to his father. "Can't we ride on the rims, Dad?"

Mr. Hollister felt that the roads were too rutted to try this. "If we had an old-fashioned car we might risk it," he said grimly, "but modern cars are slung too low to the ground."

"It's a long hike to Glendale," Pete said glumly. "We couldn't make it in less than four hours."

"Unless," Ricky added, "we knew of a short cut through the woods."

"Which we don't," his father reminded him.

Little Sue, who had been deep in thought, spoke up. "What did the bad men do with our tires, Daddy?"

Her question brought a look of hope to Mr. Hollister's face. "By George!" he exclaimed. "That's a good thought!"

146

Mr. Hollister reasoned that a few thieves could not carry all their loot through the woods. The stuff was too heavy.

"And they didn't have a car," Pete said as he glanced about the ground, "because there aren't any tire tracks."

"Then the thieves must have made off with our things over the lake," Pam deduced.

Pete snapped his fingers. "Dad, they probably wouldn't carry the tires very far for fear of being found out."

"What would they do with them then?" Mrs. Hollister wondered.

"Throw them overboard into the water," Holly declared, lifting her chin proudly at her clever reasoning.

"Yikes!" Ricky exclaimed. "In that case maybe they're not too far from shore. Let's dive down and hunt for them."

The children raced to the lake shore. Here Pete soon discovered marks left in the mud where two canoes had been launched into the water.

The children made a rush to put on their bathing togs. Then they splashed into the lake and swam out a distance. Now they began to surface-dive in an effort to locate the missing tires.

Watching from the shore, Sue giggled as she saw their heads bobbing up and down in the water. "They look like otters playing games," she said.

"Any luck yet?" Mrs. Hollister cried out to Pete, who had come up for air.

"No," he replied, "but we'll keep trying."

After they had dived for ten minutes, Mr. Hollister called to the children, "Come ashore and rest for a while."

"Okay, Dad," Pam said. Suddenly she looked about her. Pete and Ricky were swimming in, but Holly was nowhere in sight.

"Where's Holly?" Pam cried frantically.

"I saw her dive under right over there!" Mrs. Hollister cried, pointing to the left of Pam.

The other three swam quickly to the spot. Just as they reached it, Holly popped to the surface choking and sputtering.

"I——" The little girl could not talk and Pete put his arm around her and helped her reach the shore.

Mrs. Hollister patted her daughter on the back until she regained her breath. Holly blurted, "Daddy, I found the tires!"

A shout went up from the others. "Wait here," exclaimed her father who had put on his bathing trunks. "Pete and I will get them."

They swam to the spot where Holly had surfaced and dived down. Pete came up first, followed by Mr. Hollister. Each carried a tire, which they towed to shore.

"Hurrah! Hurrah!" Sue cried, dancing up and down.

"Come on, Pete, we'll get the others," Mr. Hollister said.

They dived in again. Seconds later the two surfaced, holding one tire between them. They swam to shore with it, but the perplexed looks on their faces told the others something was wrong.

"Only three tires are down there," Pete announced. "How do you like that?"

Mrs. Hollister suggested that perhaps the thieves had thrown the other two overboard farther out in the lake. "We'll look," said Pete.

This time Pam joined her father and brother as they swam out farther. They dived repeatedly but could not locate the two missing tires.

Returning to shore, the swimmers threw themselves on the ground, breathing hard from their exertion.

"Isn't it a shame!" Mrs. Hollister said. "We can't ride to Glendale on three tires."

"No. I guess we'll have to hike after all," her husband said, annoyed at the situation.

All at once Pete remembered what J.B. had told him. "Dad, let's look for the sign two hundred paces west of our camp. Maybe that will help solve our problem."

"It's worth a try anyhow," Mr. Hollister said. "We'll take a look."

As evening came on, the weary family marched into the woods, counting off the paces as they went.

"We're almost there," Pam said. "A hundred and ninety-five—ninety-six—ninety-seven——."

"Here's the sign," Holly annouced, dashing ahead. She pointed to a tree on which were fresh blaze marks.

"So this is the sign J.B. spoke of," Mrs. Hollister said. "I wonder if he made the marks just for us?"

"I think he did," said Pam. "Look!"

She pointed to a hole at the base of the tree. A brown paper bag was inside. Pete opened it.

"Sandwiches!" he exclaimed.

"Goody!" cried Holly, who was growing hungry.

As the food was shared, Pam remarked, "If J.B. left this here, he must have known the bad men were going to wreck our camp."

Just then Pete noted blaze marks on several nearby trees. "J.B. has left other signs," he said.

Pete took a bearing with his compass which he had brought along. "Crickets! This trail heads in the direction of Glendale!"

"A short cut!" Pam cried out happily. "Do you suppose J.B. knew we'd be in trouble and marked an easy way for us to reach town?"

"It wouldn't surprise me," Mr. Hollister said, as he double-checked the compass bearing.

Pete grinned. "Who's for a hike?" he asked.

It was decided that Pete and Pam should accompany their father over the trail.

"Ricky, you stay here and protect your mother and

sisters," Mr. Hollister said as they hurried back to change from their bathing suits.

"But it'll be dark before you get there," Holly said, looking worried. "How will you see?"

Fortunately both Pete and Ricky had carried flashlights attached to their belts when the family had gone to look for Scarecrow.

"We'll make out all right," Pete said with confidence. "Just don't worry."

After bidding the others good-by, Mr. Hollister and the two older children set off through the woods. The three found the trail clearly marked and well laid out as they trudged up hill and down dale making their way through the forest.

"We'll all be real woodsmen by the time we finish this camping trip," Pam declared as she stepped over a rotted timber.

"Good girl," her father praised her. He said a true woodsman never stepped on anything he could step over.

"Fallen trees may be rotten," he said, "and give way beneath you."

After a while Pete became thirsty. But there was no water in sight. "Put a few pebbles in your mouth," Mr. Hollister said. "That'll keep your throat from getting parched."

The boy found a few tiny stones on the ground which had been washed clean by the storm the night before. He popped them into his mouth and after a while said, "You're right, Dad. These are better than chewing gum."

"But don't try to bite them," Mr. Hollister said with a chuckle. He reminded the children about watching for blaze marks as they trudged along in the growing dusk.

"Especially the three marks on a tree meaning danger," he said.

"Silent signals are a wonderful thing, aren't they?" Pam mused as they climbed through a heavily-wooded glen.

Reaching the top of the rise, Mr. Hollister stopped and gazed about in all directions.

"What are you looking for, Dad?" Pete asked him.

"Smoke," he replied. "The campfire is a silent signal, too." He explained to his children that when woodsmen are in trouble and need help they build two fires close together. The two columns of spiraling smoke spell out help.

The three chatted until it became dark. After that they used flashlights and walked single file, so as not to miss any of the blaze marks.

All of a sudden Pete pointed, "Look! Three cuts in that tree!"

"Danger!" Pam exclaimed.

"Right. Let's proceed cautiously," her father said.

Keeping close to one another, they stepped gingerly ahead with Pete in the lead. Suddenly he

"Whew! That was close!"

slipped and would have fallen forward if Pam had not grabbed him.

Flashing his light down, Mr. Hollister revealed a large hole made by a tree uprooted in a storm.

"Whew! That was close," Pete said. "Thank goodness for the warning mark."

The three Hollisters stepped carefully around the pit and continued on in the darkness.

"How much farther do you think we'll have to go, Dad?" Pete asked.

"We'll know, I think, when we get to the next rise," Mr. Hollister replied. "I hope we reach town soon because I'm worried about leaving your mother and the others alone too long."

The three travelers trekked wearily up the steep slope to the next hill. Pam was first to reach the top.

"Look! Lights!" she shouted happily.

Far off in the valley below they saw a twinkling cluster of cheery yellow lights.

"That's Glendale all right," Mr. Hollister said. "J.B. certainly did show us a short cut."

Greatly encouraged, Mr. Hollister and the two children pressed forward with renewed vigor. Finally they reached the end of the woods and plodded along the main road to town. Tired and disheveled, they hurried down the main street to the warden's office.

When the trio knocked on the door, the warden let them in with a look of amazement. Quickly Mr.

Hollister told about the ruined camp and Scarecrow's disappearance and asked for help.

"I'll get a policeman and we'll go back right away," Pat Mitchell said. "We'll ride in my half-ton truck. I'll round up some supplies and car tires for you and in the meantime you folks can have something to eat. Meet you back here in about half an hour."

The Hollisters had a quick meal in a restaurant across the street, then Pam said, "Let's go to see Mrs. Blake and show her the penknife Pete has."

"Good idea," her father said.

The three hurried down the street, and despite the hour there was still a light in Mrs. Blake's house. Pete rang the bell and the woman opened the door. A look of astonishment crossed her face. After a few minutes of conversation Pete produced the knife.

"Do you recognize this, Mrs. Blake?" he asked.

As she turned it over in her hand, Mrs. Blake's eyes came alight with hope. "It's Jim's! It's Jim's penknife," she said, and explained that her husband had given it to the boy on his birthday.

Pam told where they had found the knife and of Pete's meeting in the woods with J. B.

"Now I know it's Jim," said the woman. "Please bring him back to me," she begged.

"We will," Pam promised. Then they said good-by and hurried from the house.

By the time the Hollisters reached the warden's

office a good-sized truck, its motor running, stood at the curb. The rear of the truck was packed with tires, tents, and other provisions.

Pat Mitchell, who sat in the driver's seat, introduced the Hollisters to two men who came up at this moment to join the group.

"This is Sergeant Barrett of our local police and Ranger Sharp," he said. "They're going with us."

"Sharp!" Pete repeated in surprise. He quickly told of the ranger they had met by this name.

"He's an imposter. I'm looking for him," said the tall ranger.

Sharp said that he had been ill recently for a few days. While at a friend's home recuperating, one of his uniforms and his identification card had been stolen from his bedroom.

Pat Mitchell asked the Hollisters to sit in the front of the truck with him. The two officers would ride in the back. Pam had to sit on her father's lap.

The truck sped through the town and along the main highway toward the turnoff which led to Spruce Forest. Pam drowsed along the way, weary from the long trek they had made. Finally Pete said:

"The turnoff is just ahead."

The vehicle slowed down and turned onto the narrow, rutted road through the woods. Its headlights stabbed into the blackness as it bounced and lurched along. Now and then a deer bounded across the road.

Pam watched for a while until sleep numbed her

senses again. As her head drooped forward, Pam suddenly heard her father cry out:

"Watch for the sharp bend!"

Almost at once the truck bumped and swayed, its two right wheels slipping off the road into a shallow ditch. The car door was flung open.

Pam suddenly felt herself flying through space!

CHAPTER 16

A YELLOW CLUE

PAM HOLLISTER was thrown to the side of the road, landing in a clump of tall grass. She lay stunned for a moment. Then as the girl revived, she realized her father was picking her up.

"Pam, are you all right?" Mr. Hollister asked anxiously, as he carried his daughter to the road. "You bounced right out of my arms."

Pam stood up and blinked as flashlight beams played upon her. "I—I guess I am, Dad," she replied.

Pat Mitchell said it was lucky the girl was completely relaxed when she was thrown out of the truck. This had kept her from being injured.

The four men lifted the wheels out of the ditch, setting the truck back on the road. The fire warden drove very slowly to avoid another accident.

It was nearly midnight by the time the long yellow beams of the headlights poked through the trees, revealing the Hollisters' camp. A huge fire blazed and crackled. Pete, Pam, and their father jumped out of the truck and raced ahead.

Nobody could be seen around the campfire!

A chill of fear made Pam shudder. Had the strange men come there and kidnaped the rest of the family?

"Elaine!" Mr. Hollister called out. "Holly, Sue, Ricky, where are you?"

A low growl issued from the fringe of woods and Zip bounded out. He was followed by the children and their mother.

"Oh Daddy!" Holly cried as she raced into her father's arms. "We're so glad it's you!"

"Yes, thank goodness!" her mother exclaimed as she embraced her husband.

Mrs. Hollister explained that, not knowing who was driving up to their camp, she and the children had hidden in the shadows until she had made certain that all was safe.

The fire warden introduced the ranger and the policeman. Then everyone helped unload the tents, supplies, and tires from the truck.

While the men fitted the tires to the rims of the car, Pete and Ricky set up the large tent and Mrs. Hollister and the girls prepared a tasty snack. Seated around the campfire, they ate the food and discussed the forest mystery.

"We'll go look for the poachers as soon as daylight comes," the warden said. "Our thanks to all you Hollisters for picking up the clues and notifying us."

Mr. Sharp spoke up. "I'd like to lay my hands on that scoundrel who impersonated me."

As Mrs. Hollister poured another cup of coffee for Officer Barrett, she said, "I'm glad we've been of help to you. But now I think we'd better return to Shoreham while you round up these dangerous criminals."

Hearing this, Pete nearly dropped his cocoa. "Please, Mother, we can't do that," he said pleadingly. "We want to be in on the capture."

"Oh yes," Pam chimed in. "Don't forget, Mother, we have to find Jim Blake and Scarecrow too."

"And the articles stolen from *The Trading Post* and our camp here," said Mr. Hollister.

His wife smiled at him. "What do you think, John?"

"I know it's dangerous, Elaine," he replied, "but we now have the protection of the police."

Officer Barrett spoke up. "You can depend on us, ma'am. Besides, I think we'll need your help in the roundup. The more people we have searching for these fellows, the better chance we have of finding them."

"All right," Mrs. Hollister said. "We'll do our best."

Hearing this, Ricky grinned broadly and Holly added, "Mother, you're a good detective, too."

Sue had been quiet all this time. When Mrs. Hollister glanced in her direction, she saw her small daughter lying on the ground beside Zip, sound

160

asleep. Her head was propped up against the lovely collie's back, and a relaxed smile turned up the corners of her mouth.

"The little girl," said Pat Mitchell softly, "had quite a day."

Mr. Hollister picked Sue up in his arms and carried her to the tent which had ample room for the entire family. The warden, the ranger, and the policeman said they would take catnaps in the truck, with one man standing guard until daybreak.

In spite of only six hours' sleep the Hollisters awakened eager for the search. After a hearty breakfast Warden Mitchell said:

"Sergeant Barrett, Ranger Sharp, and I have been talking things over. We'll divide into two parties." He suggested that Mr. Hollister, Ranger Sharp, and the policeman look for the poachers while the warden and the rest of the family looked for more clues at Scarecrow's shack.

Mitchell had a walkie-talkie which he would take along. In case of trouble he could communicate with his office and get more help.

As soon as he had strapped the walkie-talkie to his back, he started along the trail toward Scarecrow's cabin. The rest of his group followed. Mr. Hollister waved good-by, then he joined the two officers and headed in the opposite direction.

Zip, undecided which group to join, finally caught up with Holly. Arriving at Scarecrow's cabin, she showed the warden where they had found the tracks leading to the lake shore.

Mitchell bent down to examine them carefully. Looking up he asked, "Did you say Scarecrow was limping?"

"Yes."

"These tracks," the warden said, "were made by two men walking normally. I can't understand what happened to Scarecrow."

"Maybe they carried him away," Ricky guessed.

"I doubt it," the forester replied. "The shoe tracks aren't deep enough."

Pam looked thoughtful, then spoke up. "Maybe it was only a decoy," she said. "Perhaps Scarecrow was led off through the woods instead."

Pat Mitchell praised the girl for her clever deduction and said they would look immediately for other tracks to the woods. Retracing their steps to the bunkhouse, the group began a search for a new set of prints.

Pam noticed a long log which stretched from the rear of the hut to a tangled thicket. "Those men could have walked on this log without making tracks," she suggested, running the length of the log.

Reaching the end of it, she gave a little shriek and bent down to pick up a yellow blaze mark. "Scarecrow had a pocket full of these, remember?" she cried out.

The warden nodded approval. "I think we've found the trail," he said, pushing through the

162

"A bear! A bear!"

underbrush. A moment later he declared, "This is it! Here's another yellow disk!"

Now the picture became clear to the searchers. Scarecrow had been carried off through the woods. Unknown to his captors, he had dropped the yellow disks along the way to mark his trail.

The warden advised the Hollisters to proceed as quietly as possible. "You can't tell when we may come upon these rascals. We'll stick close together."

Ricky, Holly, Pam, and Pete were slightly in the lead. By the time they had gone a quarter of a mile, they had recovered fifteen of the yellow markers.

"That's good work," said Mitchell.

Coming to an area of large boulders interspersed with gaunt, dead walnut trees, the warden called a halt. "Now we must figure out which direction those fugitives took."

As he searched the ground over a wide area looking for footprints, Holly scrambled to the top of a boulder and peered into the tangled brush below. Suddenly she heard a rustling sound.

"Maybe it's a fawn," she thought and jumped to the ground on the far side of the boulder. Parting the bushes with her two hands, Holly peeked into a cavelike opening. A moment later she screamed at the top of her lungs and raced back.

"A bear! A bear!" she cried fearfully. "He growled at me!"

The Hollisters looked to Pat Mitchell for protection. He seemed more perplexed than alarmed.

"There hasn't been a bear in these parts for ten years," he remarked. "Where did you see it, Holly?"

"Over th-there," she said, pointing.

"Show me."

Holly climbed across the boulder with the warden at her side. Pointing out the thicket she said, "He's right in there."

There was a growling sound from within, then the huge head of a brown bear reared itself out of the bushes. Then two paws raised up, clawing the air in the direction of the searchers.

"Stand back!" the warden ordered.

As he stalked cautiously toward the bushes, the huge head turned and the bear disappeared. There was a crashing noise in the brush.

As Ricky sprang to the warden's side, he saw something lying on the ground just beyond them.

"Yikes! Look at this!" he cried out.

A few feet away lay a bearskin. Its huge brown head was cocked at a ridiculous angle.

"A phony bear!" said Ricky.

As Mitchell bent down to examine the hide, the other Hollisters crowded around. Looking up, the warden smiled. "Somebody was trying to scare us," he said. "Perhaps he didn't figure on a warden being along to protect you, so he ran."

"Who could have done such a thing?" Mrs. Hollister asked.

The warden replied that whoever the person was

he evidently had no idea the Hollisters had gone to town for help and come back so quickly.

"Mother," Pam said, "do you think that might have been Jim Blake trying to frighten us away?"

Before she could reply, Mitchell said, "If it was, we'll catch him. But we must hurry!"

CHAPTER 17

SMOKE SIGNALS

RELIEVED that the bear was not a live one, the Hollisters followed the warden in an attempt to catch up with the imposter.

"He certainly made a quick getaway," Mitchell remarked.

The children continued to find trail blazers. As they walked through a patch of towering spruce trees, Pam asked the fire warden where they were.

"We're near the shore of the lake," he said. "Right under the fox's jaw."

This made Holly giggle. "Maybe we're tickling the fox," she said.

Pete stopped to pick up another yellow disk dropped by Scarecrow. As he did, Ricky took the lead, climbing up the long slope. Reaching the top first, he turned and called to the others.

"Look! Smoke signals!"

Two white plumes rose into the air some distance ahead.

"That means trouble!" Pete cried.

The warden agreed. "Sure is the signal," he said.

"Oh, I hope Mr. Lehigh isn't hurt," said Mrs.

Hollister as they ran in the direction of the twin fires.

Presently they came to a small clearing.

"Yikes!" Ricky called out in amazement. "There's Dad and Mother's tent!" Beside it lay a pile of supplies which had been stolen from the Hollisters' camp.

The warden raced forward and looked inside the tent. No one was there.

Pete began a search through the material and discovered that the Geiger counter and his father's canoe were missing. Then he glanced at the two spiraling columns of smoke which came from the woods some distance beyond the clearing.

"We can come back for these things later," he said. "If somebody's in trouble, we ought to find out."

The warden agreed and the party pressed on. Mitchell said he surmised that the loot had been ferried down to the end of the lake and then lugged to this secluded spot.

"We're hot on their trail now!" he added jubilantly.

Now they could smell the smoke of the fires, which spurred everyone on. Presently they saw the two piles of smoking embers, situated about thirty feet apart in front of a craggy rock formation.

"Hello there!" the warden cried out. "Is anybody in trouble?"

There was no answer. But Zip, who had run over

to the rocks, now sniffed at a small opening at the base of the pile. The dog whined and barked sharply.

"Something's in there!" Holly said. "What is it, Zip?"

The dog bounded back to the girl, then retraced his steps to the small cave.

"He certainly is telling us something," Mrs. Hollister said.

"Maybe a real bear is inside," Sue ventured.

The warden walked over to one of the fires, grasped the unburned end of a smoking stick and threw it into the hole. "If an animal is in there, we'll smoke him out," he said.

For a few moments everyone waited tensely. Then from inside the cave came the sound of coughing.

"A man is in there!" Mrs. Hollister gasped.

"Come out," Ricky called, "and surrender!"

When no one emerged and the coughing continued, Pete said, "Somebody must be in trouble, Mr. Mitchell. I'll crawl in and see."

"It may be a ruse," said Mitchell. "I'll go myself."

On hands and knees he crawled into the cave. It became larger once he was inside and the warden could stand up. As his eyes became accustomed to the dim light, he called back to the others:

"There are three men in here and they're bound and gagged. Someone help me get them out."

Instantly Pete and Ricky pulled themselves into the cave and untied the nearest prisoner. As Pete ripped off the gag, he cried out:

169

"Come out and surrender!"

"Jim Blake!"

"And here's Scarecrow!" Ricky said as he bent over the second person. The third was a stranger.

"Thank goodness you got here," said Scarecrow. "I wondered if you'd find my trail markers."

As he and Jim Blake stood up, the boy said, "This other man is my father. We'll have to help him out. He's ill."

With the assistance of Pete and the warden Jim Blake carried his father through the cave opening to the sunlight outside. Mrs. Hollister and the girls were aghast at what they saw. Roy Blake had a heavy growth of beard and his sandy hair was long and disheveled. His tattered clothing covered a thin, gaunt frame.

Mrs. Hollister could tell immediately by the flushed color on his cheekbones that he was feverish. The man lay on the ground, unable to do more than groan.

"What's been going on here?" Mr. Mitchell asked.

Jim spoke up. "I can tell you all about it now. Two months ago my father and I were in a canoe on Whirlpool River. It was wrecked and Dad was badly hurt. We managed to get to shore. But we were immediately seized by three men."

"The poachers?" Pete asked.

Jim nodded. "They're market hunters. Besides, they're looking for uranium."

"Did they find any?" Pam asked.

171

"I think so."

Jim said that the three men had made them prisoners after he and his father had seen their pile of slaughtered animals.

"How did you get loose?" the warden asked.

"They didn't tie me very well. I almost got to town but they caught me. One of the men said they would hurt Dad if I tried to leave the woods again or gave anyone information. They kept Dad a prisoner in the cave but let me loose to cook for them. That's how I was able to warn the Hollisters to go back to town.

"Then this morning," Jim continued, "when I came to the cave, I found Mr. Lehigh here too. The market hunters were afraid he knew too much. So they kidnaped him and left him in the cave."

"Who are these fellows?" Mitchell said.

"Keys Craven is one of them," Jim answered.

"That's a funny name," said Holly.

"Keys is his nickname," Jim went on, "because he's a locksmith and a burglar."

"A burglar!" Pete exclaimed. "Say, could he be one of the men who robbed *The Trading Post*?"

"I think he was. I heard them mention that name."

"Where is he now?" Mrs. Hollister inquired.

Jim said that Keys had come past a few minutes before, as the boy was building two smoke signal fires to call for help. "He tied me up, saying he'd decided it was too dangerous for me to be loose while he went to town. I guess he didn't know that the fires were signals or he would have put them out."

"Which direction did Craven take?" the warden asked.

"I guess he followed the old blazers," said Jim.

The warden started off immediately. "I must capture him before he finds out we're here or he might not come back."

"I'll help you," Pete volunteered. "Come on, Zip, old boy!" The two dashed into the woods with the dog.

Mrs. Hollister and the others meanwhile tended to Roy Blake. Taking water from Jim's canteen she bathed the man's face and made him as comfortable as possible until her son and the warden came back.

"Keys is no woodsman," Jim remarked. "They ought to catch him easy even though he does have a head start."

Far off in the forest Zip's barking could be heard, growing fainter and fainter. Then suddenly it stopped.

"I wonder what happened?" Pam asked nervously.

After waiting anxiously for ten minutes, they saw Zip come jumping out of the bushes. Behind him were Pete and the warden, holding fast to a rumpled-looking man.

Holly shrieked. "That's the fake Mr. Sharp!"

"It sure is," Pete said as Warden Mitchell tied up

173

the fellow with the rope that had been used to bind Jim's father.

Keys Craven glowered at the Hollisters, then glanced down at his ripped trouser leg. "You and your dog are to blame for this!" he said. "I'll get you for this!"

"Not a chance," said Warden Mitchell.

Pete chuckled. "Zip gave him a bad time." Then he looked at the prisoner. "You're lucky he didn't bite you," he said, "after you kicked him."

The warden told of their chase through the woods after Keys. They had caught sight of the fugitive when he stepped on a fallen log instead of over it. The wood had crumbled and sent the man sprawling.

"And Zip held Keys until we could seize him," Pete added.

The prisoner was bound hand and foot and the warden set him with his back against a tree. "Now speak up!" he ordered. "Where are those two pals of yours?"

The man glared at the warden, his eyes full of hate. "I won't tell you a thing!" he hissed. "Jake and Frenchy can take care of themselves!"

"*Frenchy!*" Pam cried.

A worried look came over the prisoner's face. He realized he had said too much.

"I'll bet all three of them were responsible for the burglary of our store!" Mrs. Hollister said hotly.

They plied Keys with more questions, but he remained glumly silent.

"Well, come on," the warden said. "We'll have to get Mr. Blake to town as soon as possible. We'll return to your camp first, Mrs. Hollister."

"Scarecrow and Pete," he added, "you two can guard Keys on the way back. Untie his feet so he can walk. I'll carry Mr. Blake."

With Mrs. Hollister and Pam assisting, the warden lifted the sick man onto his back and they all started along the trail.

As they did, Keys leered at his captors. "You're in danger because you caught me," he said. "Just watch."

"What do you mean by that?" Mrs. Hollister asked.

The answer came immediately. There was a faint crackling sound from the woods. It grew louder. Then a column of black smoke rose high in the air.

"The woods are on fire!" Pam shrieked.

CHAPTER 18

THE MYSTERY SOLVED

HOT EMBERS were carried high into the air amid billowing clouds of smoke.

"I said you were in danger. Serves you right," Keys gloated.

"Oh dear," Holly said fearfully. "The poor forest animals will be burned!"

"We're all in trouble for that matter," the warden said grimly. "Keys, did you set that fire?"

"No. But maybe a cigarette I threw away did it." He gave an ugly laugh.

The warden laid the sick man down and said, "Pete, please bring the walkie-talkie here."

When it was handed to him, Mitchell spoke into the microphone. "Calling the fire tower," he said. "Smoke jumpers, hurry! A big blaze right at the fox's head. Hurry! We haven't a boat and we may be trapped!"

A moment later the reply came clearly. "Smoke jumpers on their way, Mr. Mitchell."

"Roger," he replied and handed the walkie-talkie to Pete.

The warden picked up Roy Blake and with the others hurried in the direction of the lake. Mitchell explained that teams of flying fire fighters were located at a small airport near Glendale.

"They should be in the air in a few minutes," he said, as the crackling of the flames grew louder.

Suddenly a beautiful buck raced past them. Then came rabbits, chipmunks, and groundhogs, seeking the safety of the water.

The warden kept glancing toward the sky. "I hope those jumpers come soon!" he murmured.

Just as the party reached the lake, they could hear the drone of airplanes overhead.

"Oh look!" Sue cried, pointing upward.

Parachuters jumped from three airplanes and floated down near the fire area. The Hollisters could see that they carried tanks of chemicals on their backs, along with shovels.

Half a dozen of the men landed between the Hollisters and the fire and immediately began to fight the blaze. By now the campers could feel the heat of the fire.

The warden put Mr. Blake down on a grassy spot, then rushed to direct his men in extinguishing the blaze. Suddenly a baby rabbit scampered toward Sue, who was standing on the shore. She picked the cuddly creature up in her arms.

"Don't worry, little bunny," she said. "You'll be able to go back to your home after a while."

Soon the noise of the flames decreased and the hot blast grew milder. Half an hour later the warden returned, his face covered with soot.

"The blaze is under control now," he said, "but my men will stay around the rest of the day to make sure the fire is entirely out. We can go on to your camp now, Mrs. Hollister."

As they trekked back through the woods, skirting the burned area, the warden praised Scarecrow for having dropped the yellow disks. "Without them, we might never have found you," he said.

Everyone was happy except the prisoner. Once he tried to lag behind, but Zip, barking at his heels, caused the man to quicken his steps.

Finally the weary group reached the Hollister camp site. Immediately the children's mother went for a first-aid kit and gave Mr. Blake a tablet to reduce his fever.

"I only hope he doesn't have pneumonia," she whispered to Pam.

Pete, standing near the warden, said, "I wonder how everything is going with Dad and the others?"

"Perhaps I can find out." Mitchell contacted the fire tower on his walkie-talkie. Everyone listened intently to the conversation.

"Have you heard from Mr. Hollister?"

"He's in town with Sharp and the sergeant."

"How did they make out?"

The onlookers cheered.

"Fine. They have two prisoners, Frenchy and Jake. Brought them here in the Hollisters' car."

Hearing this, the children shouted gleefully. "Hurray!" Ricky cried, jumping up and down. "All the crooks have been caught!"

Warden Mitchell asked the fire tower to communicate with Dr. Rice in Glendale. "Tell him we have a patient coming in right away. I'll bring Mr. Blake in the truck."

"Blake?"

"Roy Blake. He's safe, but ill. His son has been rescued too."

"Great, Warden. I'll tell the police to notify Mrs. Blake."

"That's all," the warden said.

A chuckle came over the walkie-talkie. "That's plenty, Mitchell!"

The sick man was helped into the back of the truck, and wrapped in blankets. Keys was pushed into the cab of the truck, secure between Warden Mitchell and Scarecrow. The Hollisters piled into the back, and the warden set off toward Glendale.

When they reached it, Pam said, "Why are all these people here?"

"Word spreads quickly in a small town," Mitchell replied. "I guess they're glad the mystery of the Blakes was solved."

The onlookers cheered as the truck drove down the street and stopped in front of the doctor's office.

Mrs. Blake was waiting there beside the physician and wept as she embraced her son and husband. Mr. Blake was carried inside, then the warden drove on.

"Now we'll turn our prisoner over to the police. His pals are waiting for him."

Mitchell drove to the back of the town hall where the police station was located and everyone went in. There they were greeted by Mr. Hollister, Ranger Sharp, Sergeant Barrett, and Police Chief Brown. As the prisoner was led away by a policeman, Mr. Hollister explained how his party had caught Frenchy and Jake making a dash for the main highway.

Sergeant Barrett spoke up. "They've confessed everything. You'll find your canoe in the bushes by the lake under the fox's jaw."

The police chief told the Hollisters that the three men had been carrying on their market hunting expedition secretly. During this time Jake, who had done some uranium prospecting in the West, discovered what looked like uranium ore.

"And wanted to dig for it right away," Pete guessed. "They needed Geiger counters, so they stole some from Dad."

"That's right," the chief replied. "They came to Shoreham because they were following Mr. Tucker. They thought that by capturing him they could keep him away from Spruce Forest. But they lost track of him the day before he visited *The Trading Post*."

The chief went on. "When the thieves saw the

181

sign in your window advertising Geiger counters, they decided to steal some."

"And used master keys to open our door?" Ricky asked.

"Yes, they did." Captain Brown said that the fellow nicknamed Keys had a large collection of keys which could open almost any lock.

"Frenchy was the ringleader," Chief Brown added. "We took this Geiger counter from him."

"Who put up the scarecrow in the road?" Pam wanted to know.

"Jake. He rigged up a hidden loudspeaker to broadcast the warning and send you home." The chief smiled. "But he didn't reckon on you Hollisters being so brave."

"Scarecrows don't frighten us," said Holly. "Some are real nice like Mr. Lehigh. He was a mystery, too."

Mrs. Hollister smiled. "Our children will never give up until they have solved a mystery."

Chief Brown grinned. "You've solved two scarecrow riddles," he said. "I'm proud of you."

Before the Hollisters left the police station, Mrs. Blake arrived to report that her husband's illness was not so serious as they had feared.

"The doctor says he'll be well in a week or two," she said happily. Then she invited the Hollister family and Scarecrow to have supper at her home that evening.

"Please come," Jim said happily. "We'll have a victory feast!"

Later, when the group gathered around the dining table in Mrs. Blake's modest home, the doorbell rang. Jim jumped up to answer it. A handsome man asked for the Hollisters.

"Come right in, sir," Jim said. "Who shall I say is calling?"

"Mr. Tucker."

The Hollister children greeted the man excitedly as Jim brought him into the dining room. When he had been introduced to Mrs. Blake and Mr. Lehigh, Jim's mother said, "Please sit down and join us."

"Well thank you. I will."

After Mr. Tucker had taken his place, the elderly professor spoke up. "I must apologize to you for living in your preserve. I had no idea it was private property."

The owner of Spruce Forest smiled. "It turned out to be a good thing you were there!"

As the jolly meal concluded, Mr. Tucker said he had heard about the forest fire and had flown up immediately. He was amazed to hear all that had happened.

"What an exciting adventure for a vacation!" he declared with a chuckle. "And I understand those poachers discovered uranium on my property." He turned to Mr. Lehigh. "You say you were a professor? What was your subject?"

"Geology."

"Fine. You're just the man I'll need to help me develop my uranium deposits."

Sue started to clap and the rest joined in. Mr. Tucker waved down the applause. "All the credit goes to the Hollisters. They certainly helped a lot of people the past few days. And the uranium will be of great assistance to our government."

Tears came to Mrs. Blake's eyes as she put an arm around her son who was seated next to her. "But the greatest treasures they found," she said, "are my boy and his father."

Scarecrow rose from his chair, holding up his glass of water. The old gentleman's eyes were full of appreciation as he said, "I want to propose a toast. Here's to the happiest family of all—the Happy Hollisters!"